SPARK OF ATTRACTION

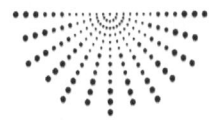

LEAH BRAEMEL

SOMERLANE PUBLISHING

Cover art by Love the Cover

Editing by Oopsie Daisy Edits

First print edition 2023

ISBN (paperback) 978-1-7389451-1-5

SPARK OF ATTRACTION

Malcolm

I always keep my promises. Like the one I gave to my best friend that I'd never date his little sister, Ellie. While I got my electrician's license and started my own business in my hometown, Ellie moved away to the city and got married. Now Ellie has returned to Port Paxton and discovered the house she's moved into has electrical problems, so I'm the first one she calls. That's when the sparks really fly. Looks like my promise is about to go up in smoke.

Ellie

When I moved away from Port Paxton to the city, I thought I'd like the opportunities, the festivals, the faster pace. I quickly learned city life could also be lonely. Now I've moved back to my hometown and into a gorgeous Victorian house. When my secret high-school crush, Malcolm Walsh, walks in to solve my electrical issues, a spark of attraction flares between us. But will that spark grow into a smoldering long-term romance? Or will it sputter and fade away?

CHAPTER ONE

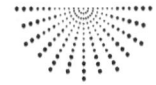

ELLIE

With a groan and a muttered curse, I rolled out of bed. Had I slept at all? I synced my watch to the app on my phone. Not even four hours of sleep, and even that wasn't in one block. No wonder my eyes scratched and burned.

"I'll love living back in Port Paxford," I'd assured everyone when I inherited the house and announced I'd be moving into it. "I'll sleep better there. There are no horns honking at three AM, no footsteps stomping on the floor above."

As I'd predicted, I'd slept well the first night I'd moved in. Probably because I'd been so exhausted from carrying boxes out of the storage unit and into the moving truck I'd rented, then out of the moving truck and onto the porch, and up the stairs to the various bedrooms. I'd set a personal best for steps and I'd even earned a daily stair-climbing award.

The second night, I'd slept well, too, thanks to a day spent vacuuming and dusting all the rooms, steam cleaning the carpets, as well as setting up the front bedroom to temporarily use as my office before doing more unpacking. By nine o'clock I'd fallen in to bed exhausted, something totally unheard of for this night owl.

Until around midnight when I'd awoken to a scritch-scratch sound.

Old houses, I discovered, make noises. Weird noises. Creaks and groans. They have trees whose branches brush against the outside walls, the roof, the windows, like a witch's nails scratching to get in. Then the sound changed locations. The wind had shifted and a different branch brushed up against the side of the house, that's all, I told myself.

I'd turned on my side, but sleep eluded me. Turned onto the other side. Was that a pitter-patter of tiny feet running across the roof? Or in the attic?

That's when I'd gotten up and tugged on the first set of clothes I could find. After turning on all the lights so I could trace the sound, I returned with no answers. Deciding not to undress in case I had to get up again in a hurry, I flopped down on the mattress, intent on falling back asleep. But I couldn't stop listening for the next creak, groan, or scratch. I would rather have been listening to clog dancers in an apartment above than thinking I had mice.

First thing I needed to do was get a cat. Or hire an exterminator. Probably both.

No. The first I needed to make a big-ass mug of coffee. It was still dark when I stumbled down to the kitchen, filled the kettle from the tap. After I plugged it in to the outlet beside the microwave, I opened up my laptop and pulled up the *House Repairs* spreadsheet I'd created. Top of my "Needs to Be Done Right the Hell Now" list was having the roof reshingled. I added a "hire an exterminator" entry above that. Which also moved "get the floors finished" and "paint the bedroom, living room and hallways" to third and fourth places, above another dozen tasks that I needed to tackle aside from remodeling the kitchen.

As a cardinal sang from the mountain ash past my back door, and chickadees and nuthatches flitted about the birdfeeder I'd hung yesterday, I frowned at my growing list of contractors I needed to contact. Then the list of contractors I'd contacted already, most of whom hadn't responded to my inquiries. Would I have as many problems finding a chimney sweep, or a painter to paint all the rooms, including the stairwell? Would the contractor I'd need to hire to take out the wall between my kitchen and dining room also be able to repair the porch? Or did that require a different tradesperson? And what order did each task need to be done? Should I get the rooms painted before I had the floors refinished or after?

Was Joshua right? Was I taking on too much?

No, this was my dream. And I'd figure it out.

I'm smart. I'm capable. I can do this.

Once I had my morning caffeine fix.

After setting my French press beside the almost-boiling kettle, I grabbed the leftover slices of pizza out of the fridge, put them on a plate and slid them into the microwave. I tapped the settings I wanted and pressed the Start button.

Sparks shot out of the outlet and smoke curled around the plugs, while an awful burning scent filled the air. I jumped back with a shriek so high-pitched, I'm surprised it didn't break all the glasses on the counter.

The first call I made that morning was not to an exterminator. Or a roofer. I called Malcolm, my brother's best friend, and the only electrician I knew.

CHAPTER TWO

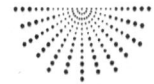

MALCOLM

I poked at the scorched outlet, the plastic covering slightly puckered and blackened. "You say the kettle was running when you turned on the microwave?"

"That's right," Ellie agreed. "Then there was this really loud pop and sparks shot out. Was it the microwave what caused it? Or the kettle? Do I need to contact a manufacturer or see if there's a recall or something?"

"I don't think it's the kettle or microwave's fault." Given the age of the kitchen, I had my suspicions of what I would find once I opened up the outlet.

When my best friend Josh mentioned Ellie was moving back to Port Paxton, he'd told me he thought his sister had rose-colored glasses about Hauser House and the amount of work it would require.

I'd learned from years of experience, both apprenticing and in my own business, that hundred-year-old houses could come with a shit-ton of problems hidden behind their fancy wainscotting and crown moulding. Sometimes you had to admit it was a lost cause, and stick a *For Sale* sign on the lawn.

I didn't see any issues screaming for immediate attention. The air was stale, like old people and cleaning fluids, but nothing a couple of nice spring days with the front and rear windows left wide open wouldn't fix. The faded hallway paint had rectangular spots that hinted at pictures that had been removed, which was a cosmetic issue easily remedied with a can of paint. Soot stains above the marble fireplace in the front room could mean there had been a chimney fire that might have cracked flue tiles that needed replacing, or it might mean a badly designed flue fireplace that didn't properly direct the smoke. Either could be a pricey fix. Or maybe the soot was simply an accumulation of over 130 years of wood fires and, like the hallway, the mantel and wall simply needed to be repainted.

The scuffed wooden floors in both the hallway and main room, probably oak, which I suspected had once shone, needed a complete refinishing. It wouldn't scare me off, but maybe Josh, who had grown up in a more modern house, saw such things as problems?

Unlike her brother, I understood why Ellie loved this old Victorian house. It was warm, solid, and inviting. Few modern houses had eleven-foot ceilings, transoms over the internal doors or decorative plasterwork, including rosettes around the art deco chandeliers like the one in the hallway. Fewer still had stained glass around the original oak doors, or their original crown moulding. And only Hauser House had nearly a full acre that sat on a hill with a lush lawn that sloped down to Hawkeshead Lake and was bordered by ancient lilacs, maples and cedars.

Although I'd avoided facing Ellie, I finally turned, forcing myself not to react to her outfit.

Her hair, which had been visible-from-the-space-station orange in high school, had darkened to a reddish brown. She'd pulled it into something my sister called a messy bun. I wasn't sure if it was messy because she'd deliberately styled it that way or if she'd slept in it and hadn't brushed her hair yet. The manufacturer's tag that should be at the back of her neck sat at the notch of her collarbone, the seams visible along the shoulders and down the sleeves. Her multicolored pants were also inside out. I considered the plausible reasons for her outfit.

"Have you been having any other electrical issues? Do I need to check out the lights in your bedroom?"

She narrowed her eyes at me and scowled. "My bedroom is just fine, thank you."

Shit. "I'm not planning to..." I swallowed the first word that jumped onto my tongue and substituted, "get into your bed." I waved my hand at her outfit. "I figured you couldn't see when you were getting dressed. If your lights aren't working upstairs, I can look at them, too."

Ellie glanced down and shrieked the word I'd self-censored, then raced out of the kitchen, papering her path with more f-bombs and a few s-bombs too. Her rapid thump-thump-thump up the stairs and along the hallway traced her path. The dishes in the cabinet behind me rattled as she slammed shut the door directly above the kitchen.

Before I'd stuck my size-ten steel-toed boot in my mouth, I'd intended to ask her where I'd find the fuse box. Without being able to ask her, I figured the basement was a safe place to start.

Hauser House had been built in the days when they laid stone walls with slate slabs over packed earth. A single incandescent bulb swung from the middle of the room, casting long shadows over everything. Creepy. But going into people's basements, whether modernly finished or ancient pits like this one, was part of my job. To be honest, it wasn't the worst basement I'd been in. That honor belonged to my grandparent's old farmhouse, which may be why I have a fear of old basements even now.

Luckily, the basement was empty, so I didn't have to move piles of furniture or boxes to get to the fuse box tucked behind a newish gas furnace. Since the light didn't reach this corner, I shone my flashlight over the fuse panel.

After assuring myself that Ellie had turned off the main power, I leaned in closer, examined the fuses, and removed several, muttering, "What the fuck?"

I doubted old Mrs. Hauser, the previous owner, had screwed in these fuses. From what Joshua had told me, she'd been an old lady who hadn't been able to manage stairs for years. Which meant someone else had put the entire house at risk. Perhaps it had been Ellie's dead husband or maybe old Mrs. Hauser had hired some handyman who didn't give a fuck what amperage he used. Whoever had done it, if I met them, I'd sound them with my damned threading driver.

"What's wrong?"

I jumped because I hadn't heard Ellie's approach. How long had she been standing there? Had I voiced my threat aloud?

She descended the rest of the stairs, her lips pressed together in an expression totally different from any I'd been familiar with back in high school. Hesitant. Insecure? The high school Ellie I'd known had been confident, outgoing. Bubbly and chatty, always smiling. Someone had burst her bubble, changed her. Would her husband's death have done that? Or had something happened to her that had deflated her self-confidence?

High school Ellie wore pink sweatshirts with teddy bears on them, soft comfortable jeans if she was in school, or when at home, fuzzy pants, equally inscribed with teddies or bunnies, and her feet encased in fuzzy slippers complete with floppy bunny ears. Grown-up Ellie wore a dark-green t-shirt with a graphic that said "If Only Sarcasm Burned Calories" beneath a thick pink sweater that looked hand-knitted, neon purple yoga pants which clung to her curves, and—I bit back my urge to laugh—fuzzy pink slippers complete with bunny ears.

It took all my effort not to gather her in my arms and cuddle her. Tell her everything would be all right.

For a brief period in high school, I had seriously considered dating her. After a debate about the wisdom of dating my best friend's sister, I'd given in to temptation and kissed her once, planning to ask her to be my date at my prom. Two days later, her brother made me promise to never approach Ellie for the rest of my life. A blood oath too, not a simple pinky swear. I don't know if he'd seen us or if Ellie had confessed that I'd kissed her, but I'd had to make a choice between my best friend and his sister.

The ancient *bro code* won, and I'd stayed home instead of attending my prom.

In return, I'd demanded Josh make the same promise not to pursue my older sister Chantel, not that it was any hardship on his part because he and Chantel couldn't stand each other, and at the time, I suspected Chantel preferred her own gender over guys. Something she later confirmed when she brought home her college girlfriend and announced they were a couple.

But now here I was, over twenty years later, and those old feelings stirred up again, making me imagine Ellie in my bed. Me in her bed. Us getting down and dirty on the stairs. On the kitchen table. Me on top of her, her on top of me.

I faced the fuse box and, discreetly—I hoped—adjusted the fabric constricting my chubby.

However, I suspected Josh would still hold me to my promise. Plus, there was the whole dead husband issue. So no matter how attractive I found her, no matter how much I wanted to remove the scrunchie and watch her hair tumble about her shoulders, or how much I wanted to trace my tongue across her freckles and taste her delicious lips, Eleanor Mason was, and would always be, forbidden fruit.

When I faced her again, I blew out a breath, reminded myself of the promise I'd made, and swung the beam from my flashlight onto the fuse box again.

I tapped one of the dusty gray wires coming out of the box. "This is aluminum wiring. They used it back in the 70s when copper got crazy expensive." I then explained how aluminum wire contracted and expanded, causing arcing like she'd witnessed. "I can go through your outlets today and make sure everything's tight to prevent future arcing. Your outlets will need to be checked regularly, too. But Ell..." I tapped the fuse box. "This unit needs to be replaced. And soon."

Her eyes narrowed. "What's your definition of soon? This week? This summer? This year?"

"It's not an *immediate* problem, but I've been in more than one house where this exact fuse box has caught fire. I'm not trying to pressure you, but I don't want you to put it off too long."

She frowned, but nodded.

Hating to pile problems on her, but needing to address the issue, I held up one of several fuses I'd removed. "This is an easier and less expensive fix. These are 40-amp fuses, and the wiring in that outlet is for 15 amps."

Like many of my clients, Ellie's eyes clouded in confusion. "Isn't forty amps better than fifteen?"

A common misconception and her question made me wonder if she had been the one to use the wrong amperage. "Think of it like the fuse is a big pressure sprayer that pushes out water at 40 pounds of pressure, but the hose— the wire—can only handle 15 pounds pressure. Then you turned on two different devices that draw full power and the wire couldn't handle it."

Ellie focused on the fuse I was holding and frowned. "So the circuit overloaded."

"Right. Even once I fix the outlet, you can use the kettle *or* the microwave, but never in the same outlet at the same time." I frowned. "Until I've looked at how the wiring is done, you may not be able to run them together even if they're plugged into different outlets."

Her mouth curved into an O. "Grandma Ruby complained that if she ran the dishwasher and washing machine at the same time, the fuse kept blowing even though they're on different floors. Is this the same thing?"

"Without looking at the wiring for those units, I wouldn't want to make a guess. But probably." I suspected whoever had wired up the extension had put both appliances on the same circuit, too. Which wouldn't have passed code even back then. "Let's go back upstairs and we can talk about what your plans are for this place."

I trailed her up the stairs to the kitchen. Yes, I enjoyed the view of the tight fabric stretched over her enticing butt as she climbed each narrow wooden stair.

After I'd removed the outlet cover and hissed at the burnt and exposed wires, Ellie asked, "You can fix it, right?"

"I can," I replied, not liking the tremor in her voice. "It doesn't need to be replaced, but it needs to be checked for loose wires regularly. I'm surprised your insurance company didn't ask for an ESA certification."

"They may have, but I had so much going on in selling our old condo and getting Ruby's estate dealt with, I just paid them the higher price." Another frown marred her expression. "How much will it cost?"

"To fix this plug alone? Or to check all of them?"

She caught her bottom lip between her teeth. I'd forgotten she used to do that when she was considering an important question. "All of them?"

After doing a quick count of the number of outlets in

the extension, and a mental calculation about how long it would take me to check each one, I gave her a rough quote.

"How much would you charge to upgrade the fuse box?" Her voice was small, hesitant. As if her favourite doll had lost its head to an enthusiastic terrier. Which had happened when we were kids, so I knew exactly how that sounded. Almost as heartbroken as when I'd lied and told her I wasn't interested in dating her, then walked away.

CHAPTER THREE

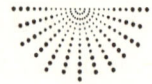

ELLIE

My stomach had twisted at Malcolm's assessment of Hauser House's wiring problems. When Josh and I had done the initial walk through after the probate had completed, Josh had told me I should sell it and buy a smaller house, one that didn't need so much work, that I should invest the leftover as a nest egg. But I've loved this house since I was a little girl. I'd stop my bike on the sidewalk and gawk at the round turret with its steep roof that resembled a castle, and the dormers, the gingerbread gables and the massive wraparound porch. When Gareth brought me to meet his grandmother shortly after we were married and I was finally invited inside, I fell in love with every inch of it. My favorite spot has always been the garden room off the kitchen. The stained-glass windows and stone slab floor with its calming dappled light have always lowered my stress levels.

I hadn't considered that the old place might need

electrical work done, other than having a few more outlets added when I had the kitchen gutted. Grandma Ruby had said they'd added the extension back in the 70s, creating a new kitchen and dining area that already needed updating. Maybe electrical work needed updating just as often?

But now as Malcolm talked about replacing the fuse box, which sounded like a major job, my gaze fell on the twisted plastic outlet on my counter and I remembered the sparks and smoke. And the acrid smell.

Had I made the wrong decision by going with my heart rather than my head?

No. I still loved this place. I wanted to bring it back to its grandeur and I had the means to afford it. With house prices the way they were these days, I doubted I'd ever get another chance to own such a beautiful home.

"I'd appreciate it if you could do up a quote for me then."

I explained my plans to him, even pulled up a sketch I'd stored on my tablet. He jotted down notes as I talked about adding air conditioning along with a generator hookup, a walk-in closet and a luxury ensuite, and how I needed additional plugs in the upstairs turret room I wanted to use as my office. "I haven't told Joshua any of this yet, so please keep this between you and me for now."

Malcolm blew out a long, slow breath and took even longer to meet my eyes. His familiar hazel gaze sent a tug deep in my chest that had me leaning toward him before I could stop myself. Why was I stopping myself? Because he'd walked away from me once already, and I didn't need that type of rejection again.

"I can do that," he said.

"Could you recommend an exterminator, too?"

That earned me a tightening of his mouth. The dark beard he now sported, which included a few threads of gray, highlighted his lips. Lips I wanted to press against mine again.

"You've seen mice?"

"I heard them," I admitted. "I think. It might have been a branch scratching against the window. I haven't slept well lately, so maybe my imagination was in hyperdrive."

"I'll look to see if I can find any entry points before I go. Do you need me to recommend some reputable roofers? Because your roof won't make it through another winter."

"I've already contacted some." Did he think I couldn't see the curling shingles, especially on the west side of the house, and know enough to realize the roof needed attention?

"I could give you a list of which ones to avoid. Joshua would give me hell if I let you hire someone incompetent."

I pushed my glasses down on my nose so I could press my thumb against a spot above my eyes that a chiropractor had said could help relieve headaches. Was he mansplaining or simply looking out for a friend? After life with Gareth, sometimes I found it hard to tell. I settled for a bland, "Thanks. I'd appreciate your advice," because he was in the business and would know who to trust.

"You haven't had your morning coffee yet, have you?" Malcolm asked, his head tilted to one side as he watched me.

"No." Ah. Caffeine withdrawal tied with sleep deprivation. No wonder I had the mother of all headaches building to an explosive pressure in my skull.

"Why don't I take you down to the Pancake Shack? You can have a coffee and breakfast, and we can talk more about your plans."

I looked down at the outfit I'd hurriedly tossed on. Pink and purple? What had I been thinking? I love bright colors, especially pink, but this combination was bizarre even for me. Then again, maybe it was an unconscious, "Fuck You, Gareth" statement since he had always insisted I dress in dark colors.

"This is much more slimming on you," he'd murmur, taking a colorful garment I chosen and replacing it with a gray, black or brown version. "Someone with your body type shouldn't wear bright colors. And someone with your hair color should never wear pink."

The week before we'd been married, Gareth had taken me to a stylist and had them tone down my hair color to a shade he found acceptable. It wasn't until I was getting dressed for his funeral that I'd realized that, much like my hair and my closet, my entire life contained absolutely no color. The next week, I'd culled most of the clothes he'd chosen for me and gone on a shopping spree to replace them with clothes in bright, happy colors. I'd let my natural hair color grow out and found my joy again. But this morning's pink and purple combination was a little too out there, even for me.

"Let me get properly dressed and I'll meet you there, okay?"

"Go. Get dressed." Malcolm's voice, like his eyes, held a warmth I'd longed for but never received from the one person who should have looked at me the way Malcolm did now. "I'll wait for you however long it takes."

Why did it sound like he wasn't talking about meeting me at a restaurant? Was I seeing a spark of attraction that I'd once thought I'd seen back in high school? Or were my own needs projecting? I'd spent too many years convinced that no one other than Gareth would ever be interested in me, so the hope that flared at the way Malcolm leaned toward me created a long-forgotten flutter in my body.

Choosing the third outfit for the day took me longer than I'd expected. By the time I picked up my purse, at least a half dozen different pairs of pants and a dozen or more tops lay on the bed, the dresser, and across the boxes I hadn't yet unpacked. I'll put them away later, I promised myself.

I stopped in the bathroom for yet another check on my makeup. After Gareth's death and with working from home for the last three years, I'd gotten out of the habit of wearing makeup unless I knew I had to be on camera for a meeting. Where it used to take me less than fifteen minutes to end up with perfectly applied eyes, lips and lashes, it took me twice as long today. I'd hesitated while deciding whether to put in my contacts that Gareth had insisted I wear in public. Ultimately, I decided this was Port Paxton and Malcolm, both of whom had seen me in my pimply, gangly teenage years, and put on my favorite purple cats-eye glasses.

Gareth wouldn't have approved of the woman who stared back in the mirror, but I was starting to like her again.

CHAPTER FOUR

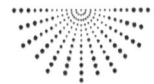

MALCOLM

Being midweek in April—in other words, when the tourists hadn't descended yet—less than a half dozen cars were parked in the Pancake Shack's lot, which meant I could grab a booth where Ellie and I could talk without a lot of people overhearing.

I wondered if Ellie realized how much work, time and money even a simple kitchen gut could take, let alone changing the configuration of the house's plumbing to give the primary bedroom an ensuite. Though she'd inherited the house and probably wasn't saddled with a mortgage, I wasn't sure how financially secure she and her husband had been before his death, or if she'd been left with a ton of debt that had wiped out any life insurance or savings they'd had, if he even had life insurance.

I grabbed my phone and called the one person who could give me an inside scoop.

"Josh speaking," he answered after the receptionist put me through.

After we shot the shit for a few minutes, I said, "I got a call from your sister this morning. She blew a fuse." I realized how that could be misinterpreted, so I added, "As in, literally."

"Let me guess. You found that there's more wrong with that dump than a blown fuse?"

Dump? Hauser House needed work but in no stretch of the imagination did I consider it a dump. Had he seen something I'd missed? I hadn't been upstairs yet. Was there some major leak that had rotted the wood floors, or gotten in behind the walls? Was there a room full of black mold?

Or did he suspect I might try to hook up with his sister again? "What specifically are you worried about?"

"Other than the roof?" There was a pause and I figured he had taken off his glasses and was pinching his nose, a habit he'd had even back in elementary school. "Look, I do numbers, not remodeling projects, but from what El told me, old lady Hauser let things go after her husband passed about ten years ago, so I'm worried you might find it needs a lot more work that I didn't notice."

A fair concern, but that he hadn't seen anything upstairs relieved some of my suspicions.

"I tried to convince her to sell it and buy something newer, that needed less work," he continued. "Something smaller so she wouldn't have so much to keep up on her own, but you know Ellie."

I did, but I stayed quiet.

"So how much is going to cost her? To fix up whatever is wrong with her wiring?"

This is where the conversation got sticky. Ellie was my client, not Josh. I'm not a doctor so there isn't anything in our relationship that means I can't discuss any problems I'd found, but it still felt like I was betraying Ellie. "I'll give her a quote and if she cares to share it with you, that's up to her."

"That much?"

"You're not my client, Josh."

He muttered something that sounded an awful lot like *fuck you*, then blew out a breath. "Okay, but don't sugarcoat things for her. Be honest, even if it means telling her the brutal truth that the place is going to be a money pit."

I stared down the main street toward the lake, picturing what I'd seen in that quick glimpse of Hauser House, making complex mental estimates. The multifaceted roof over multiple wings and bays, plus the extension, and a round tower with its steep pointed cupola would be any roofer's dream for tripling the costs of a modern two-story house. Some boards on the verandah needed replacing, but the bones of the place felt solid.

"I'll give her an estimate," I said slowly, "and I can recommend some other reputable people who will do the same. But, J-man? What are you not telling me? Does Ellie not have enough money for pay for any repairs?"

There was another long pause. "Look, don't tell this to your buddies when they're doing their quotes, but between Hauser's and his grandmother's estates? Ellie's set for life. She'd never have to work again if she invests it properly. Thing is, Mal? You know how she trusts people, always has." His voice dropped into a growl. "I'm worried people will see her bank balance and think she's fair game."

Was he warning me off too? I wasn't rich, far from it, but I made a comfortable living and wasn't buried in debt like a few of my friends. In addition to owning a moderately successful business, I owned my own home that came complete with a double garage that served as my workshop. Okay, I and the bank owned my home, but I had less than ten years left on the mortgage. Though it wouldn't compare with Hauser House for square footage, acreage, or its spectacular lake view, I didn't need anything more.

"Ell needs an unbiased opinion about whether that old place is worth saving," Josh continued. "Don't let her get taken by some con man." Someone said something in the background and he returned with a "Look, I gotta go. I've got another call coming in. Let me know how it goes."

Damn it, it sounded like Josh still expected me to treat her like a surrogate sister. Which I didn't want to do.

Down in the basement, the spark of attraction between us had lit the space between us. At least on my side. We were both unattached adults. But after my doomed relationship with Natalie, I'd learned that romantic sparks could either flare up into a bonfire or spark an ember that flickered briefly then died a slow, painful death.

I pocketed my phone and entered the diner. With a nod from Rachel, I sat at a booth in the corner. I'd worked here a busboy back in high school when Rachel started as a part-time waitress, before she'd bought out the owner to run the place herself.

"Coffee, hon?" Rachel asked, placing a white mug in front of me then filling it without waiting for an answer.

"I'm going to need another place setting too. Client's going to be joining me."

"Oh, yeah?" She rocked back on her heels and examined me as if I were a diamond ring in a store and she was appraising its value. She'd briefly been married to a jeweller and had had learned all about the 5Cs. Sounded like she'd found a way to apply her ex-husband's evaluations of his clients to her diner customers. "Big job? Or pretty client?"

Both. Not that was I about to say that to Rach.

"Big job. Potentially."

"Good for you." She handed me a menu which was an oversized laminated sheet with the breakfast and lunch menu on one side, the dinner menu on the other. She placed another mug, turned over on its saucer, on the table across from me, and set a menu beside it. "No use filling it until your client arrives, otherwise it'll get cold."

Right. "Oh, and she likes cream. A lot of it, so can you make sure you bring a bunch of those little creamers for her?"

Her eyebrows lifted at my "she" but Rachel didn't say anything before wandering away to refill the mugs of the other customers.

Rach had refilled my mug twice before Ellie slid into the booth across from me. She'd changed yet again. This time she wore tight dark-blue yoga pants with a light-blue strip down the side, with a light-pink sweater that dropped down over one shoulder, revealing a darker pink strap of a T or those lacy things women wore under their clothes. Her messy bun had been rewound so it was much more neat and professional looking, confined with a sparkly multi-coloured scrunchie. She'd added eye makeup and lipstick that had me locking my ass to the seat against the urge to lean across the table and kiss her. Again.

"Sorry to keep you waiting." With a brilliant smile, she greeted Rachel, who poured her a coffee and placed a bowl filled with creamers in the middle of the table with a wink in my direction.

Ellie poured a creamer into the coffee, then another and another. And another. Four, not eight like she'd used the last time I'd seen her. She picked up her mug, took a sip, closed her eyes and heaved an orgasmic sigh that had me wondering what sounds she'd make beneath me in bed, or on top of me, riding me.

Another sip. Another moan followed by a breathy, "I needed this."

Afraid she'd catch me staring at her, I buried my face in the menu. I'd looked it over multiple times already and knew what I was going to order but I needed a cover. She'd been cute back at her house, but with the makeup, earrings and everything, she was bloody gorgeous. And those soft sounds she kept making with each sip had me wanting to drag her out of here and take her back to her place, and not to examine the wiring.

Rachel had returned and topped up Ellie's coffee. "D'you know what you want, hon?"

I half-choked on my coffee at the answer I wanted to give. *Ellie. In bed. My face buried between her thighs so I can make her moan like that again.*

Ellie opened her mouth as if to speak, glanced at me from under her eyelashes, then caught her bottom lip between her teeth and surveyed the menu again. She closed up the menu and handed it to Rachel. "I'll have the egg-white omelette and fruit, no toast, thanks."

I couldn't stop myself from frowning. "They've got the banana bread French toast. That used to be your favorite."

She hesitated, shook her head. "Not today. Just the egg-white omelette and fruit, please."

Frowning, I said, "*I'm* having the banana bread French toast. Bacon, brown bread, buttered."

Rachel snorted. "That's what you order every time so I already put up your order." She took our menus and left us alone.

We chatted about the changes to Port Paxton since Ellie had left, the rising cost of gas and which station had the best prices, the ones in town or the ones on the highway, and, the staple of any Canadian conversation, the weather. Once the food arrived, we fell silent, and I found myself stopping to watch Ellie eat. How she precisely cut up the omelette with manners fit for Buckingham Palace. Josh and Ellie's mother had raised them to have good manners, but she was so measured in her movements, someone had obviously taken her training even further. Her husband's influence no doubt.

I followed the fork's path to her mouth, entranced by her tongue when it darted out to clean any leftovers from her lips. Her lips shone enticingly and I found myself wondering if her lipstick had a flavour or what she'd taste like without it.

She stopped, a piece of cantaloupe speared on the fork's tines halfway to her mouth, then lowered it. "What's wrong? Do I have egg on my chin or something?"

Before I could reply, she picked up the napkin and patted her chin and over her lips.

"No, you're fine. No egg on your face." I wasn't about to admit that I found watching her erotic so I settled for the simpler, "I like watching you."

Color flooded her face and she pushed her plate to the centre of the table, her omelette only half consumed.

I stared at her plate trying to see if I could tell what was wrong with it. It looked bland, but properly prepared. "Is there something wrong with your food?"

"It's fine," she muttered.

"But you've barely touched it. If there's something wrong, we can let Rachel know and she'll have Carl make you a new one. Or we can order something el—"

"*We* don't have to do anything." She snapped as she slapped her palms flat on the tabletop. "If I say I'm done eating, it's not your place to question me." After a shuddering inhale, she closed her eyes and took three deep breaths before meeting my gaze again. "I'm sorry. I shouldn't have snapped at you like that. It's just—" She shook her head. "Never mind."

Without giving me a chance to respond, she continued, as calm as if she were sitting across from me at a boardroom table. "Tell me what you think it's going to take to get my place into order electrically."

Okay, if she wanted to play things that way, I could deal. I pushed my plate to the side. "I can't give you a full estimate unless I look over the place and know exactly what I'm dealing with. Are you looking for a quick fix until you gut the kitchen? Or do you want me to figure out the cost of going whole hog and doing everything once—the kitchen, the heated towel rack in both upstairs bathrooms, and the underfloor heating in your ensuite, the whole shebang?"

"It would be cheaper to do it at all at the same time, right? Rather than paying a plumber—or an electrician—to come back multiple times?"

I leaned back against the seat. "It would be, but to do all this isn't going to come cheap."

Her lips tightened. "You've been talking to Josh."

Tread carefully. "D'you remember that Tom Hanks movie where they bought an old mansion that fell apart and they ended up mortgaging themselves to the hilt? It wouldn't take much to have that happen with this house."

"Two weeks, two weeks," she mimicked the tradesmen quoting the timeframe that ended up taking months. "But, Mal? This house? It's worth it."

She leaned forward, her eyes bright, as she again described her vision for the house. I found myself drawn into her dreams, entranced by her passion, the way her eyes sparkled as she talked, the way her hands moved, waving as if they were touching the molding, the textured plaster. Touching *me*.

The first week I started my electrical apprenticeship classes, my teacher told the students that once your friends and neighbours discovered you were an electrician, whether you were a full-fledged certified electrician or still in your first week as an apprentice, they would hit you up for free electrical work. He stressed that we had to learn to quote a price and stick to it, and that the only person whom you should say yes to doing their electrical work for free was your mother.

By the time Ellie wound down, her infectious attitude and joy in her plans for the house had infected me. I wanted to do the damned job for free, to make her dream real.

If I went back to his class now, Mr. Farquharson would definitely give me a failing grade.

CHAPTER FIVE

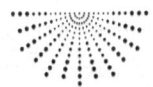

ELLIE

I don't know why I'd snapped at Malcolm when he'd suggested I order something other than the omelette. I'd wanted the French toast. I really had, but the way he was watching me made me wonder if he was like Gareth, if he would judge me for not watching my calories. Throughout my marriage, I'd strictly watched my weight and exercised with a trainer to keep myself at Gareth's declared ideal weight for my height.

As I described what I imagined for the house, I realized Malcolm wasn't watching me with judgment, but interest. Not like he was considering how much he could charge me for fixing up Hauser House, but like he wanted to strip me naked and bury his face between my thighs.

Count me in, Malcolm, because I want that too.

I'd been a widow for almost two years now, but my husband hadn't touched me for almost a year before that. So Malcolm's interest made my panties damp and I was certain if I looked down, my nipples would be standing up at attention. I squirmed in my seat against the need to feel Malcolm's touch on my back, on my belly. Inside me.

He frowned and reached across the table to cover my hand with his. "Are you all right?"

"I'm fine." I ground it out, unwilling to admit that I was ready to jump his bones right here in the diner because of his simple touch. Maybe when we got back to my place, I could lure him to my bedroom and strip him naked, beg him to fuck me hard and fast. Soft and slow would be good too.

Except when we returned to the house, he was all business. He pulled a toolbox out the back of his battered red half ton, dropped it in my front hallway, then returned to unhook a ladder and carry it inside. He spent a long time in the basement by the fuse box, then stuck a yellow box with yellow and red lights into each outlet, then opened every outlet on the main floor, *hmm*ing and muttering while making notes.

I trailed after him when he headed upstairs, waiting in the hall silently as he inspected each outlet and switch in the two spare bedrooms and made more notes. He even took photos.

I hurried after him when he opened the door to my bedroom.

"I'm not always this messy," I said, hating how weak my voice sounded.

He turned his head, and there was a hint of amusement tugging at his lips that faded when he looked at me. "I'm not judging you, Ell."

"I know." But my eyes welled up at the gentleness of his tone.

He stuck the tape measure, notebook and pencil in his tool belt, and took my hands in his, pulling me until we faced each other. "I don't think you do. Not really." He stroked a thumb over my cheek. "I get it, okay? This is your private place, your sanctuary. You weren't expecting anyone to come in here today."

Or ever.

"I am not judging you. Hell, you should see my place at the end of the week." He stroked my cheek again and I found myself leaning into his palm. "You're taking on all this work, all this responsibility on your own. You know what you want, and you're going after your dreams. Do you know how amazing you are?"

I swallowed hard against the emotion welling up at his declaration. He didn't know.

"I'm not," I whispered.

He pulled me against his chest and wrapped his arms around me, nestling my head beneath his chin. "Oh, baby, you've been through a lot. You don't have to be strong for me."

The way he whispered it, the heat sinking into my bones made me want to strip him naked and...well, do all the things Gareth had never done but I'd read about. Worse, tears filled my eyes as I realized what I'd missed out on all these years.

"What's going on in that head of yours? Talk to me, Ell."

I pulled away and paced to the window, wiping the heel of my hand over my eyes. "I'm tired, that's all."

"No, it's not all. But I'll leave it be." He left the *for now* unspoken but I heard it. When I didn't turn to face him, he sighed and asked, "Where's the attic hatch?"

I pointed down the hall. "There are a couple entrances depending on which part of the house you're in."

"Right. Look, this is going to take a while. Why don't you go downstairs and..." He scratched his head. "I was going to say make yourself a coffee, but the power's still switched off."

"I'm fine. You do what you have to do."

By the time I'd gathered myself enough to leave my bedroom, including tidying it, Malcolm trudged back upstairs in a white suit that made him look like a giant marshmallow.

I couldn't stop my snort as he pulled the hood over his head and tied it tight it, leaving only his face exposed. "Seriously? You look like you're about to go into a nuclear reactor."

He shrugged, leaned down and pulled out a respirator from his bag. "It's an old house, Ell. Who knows what I'm going to find up there. Asbestos. Mold. Mouse droppings. It's better to be safe than sorry."

I couldn't suppress my shudder as I agreed with him. While he climbed the ladder that he'd already set up beneath the hatch, I stayed at the base, even once he disappeared from sight. Boards creaked overhead, there was rustling, and a few curse words I don't think I was supposed to hear.

"Problems?" I called.

"U gog nob and oob."

Nob and Boob? Bob is rude? "What?"

He repeated it again, but it still made no sense since he was talking through his respirator from the other end of the attic.

He finally reappeared and climbed down the ladder, the white suit now a grubby gray. After he dropped his respirator into his bag and stripped off his marshmallow suit, he said, "You've got knob and tube up there."

"What's that?"

"It's the pre-1940s original wiring. Whoever rewired the house back whenever they updated it spliced in the copper wiring to go down the walls but it runs off the old stuff. Did your insurance company put a rider on your policy or offer you any incentives to remove it?"

I shook my head. "There was something about the electrical but I figured I'd get it fixed when I redo the kitchen. Is it unsafe?"

He tilted his hand back and forth. "It's not something I have to report. It can stay up there with no problems. I've even had to tap off it when the building was too complex to replace it. When you get other electricians in here to give you a quote, they may give you a hard sell to remove it all. And you could. It's totally up to how comfortable you are with it." He explained the intricacies of disconnecting the panels and tracing it back to the fuse box. Though I couldn't follow what he was talking about, I found myself soaking up his excitement. He stopped mid-sentence. "I'm losing you, aren't I?"

"You're as passionate about your job as I am about fixing up this place."

He grinned, lighting up his whole expression even his eyes. "You get it. Not many people do. But yeah, I love taking old buildings and fixing them up so they'll survive another hundred or more years."

He packed up his case. "Let's talk about this downstairs."

I followed him back to the dining room, where he took a seat and made some notes on a notepad, tapped some more into a tablet. "Okay, so I'm not a home inspector. I'm going by what I've seen at other sites. You'll need to bring in multiple people for getting this place into the shape you're wanting." He checked my list, scribbling numbers beside the tradesmen I'd need and confirmed most of what I'd already written, adding a few details I hadn't considered.

"I'm going to make a quote based on stages, okay? I'll do one for what I need do today, and what needs to be done to get the aluminum to pass if your insurance company needs documentation. You might get a better rate if you send them the forms I'll give you. I can also give you a quote for replacing the aluminum if you want, and the knob and tube if it bothers you, but really, it's fine as long as you have someone in to check the outlets regularly.

"You can fine-tune the plans once you've had a contractor in to tell you what can and can't be done about gutting the kitchen." He nodded toward the rough sketch he'd made of my dream kitchen. "You should hire a structural engineer to advise you about taking out the wall between the kitchen and dining room and putting in the proper structural support. But Ell, with what you're looking for, gutting the kitchen is going cost you $50K. Easy."

I nodded. "I'd figured it would be at least that. And don't worry, I'm good for it." And a lot more, but I was hesitant to let anyone know how much I'd inherited, otherwise they might see me as ripe for the picking and I'd find myself in another bad relationship. Or worse, out of a bad relationship with my savings drained.

"Oh, one last thing. The hydro pole partway up your driveway? That's rotting and needs replacing. It looks like it'll fall over in the next good windstorm. When you hire an electrician, make sure they put that high on the list because replacing that that could take anywhere from three days to...months, depending on if there's a pole available. Plus, you need to hire an arborist to trim the trees because a branch could take out the power line, if not the pole too."

I loved the trees lining the driveway, ancient maples that were probably a hundred years old, the cedar hedging along the roadway that had been planted when I was a kid and now towered twenty foot tall. "Wouldn't the town be responsible for the powerline?"

He shook his head. "Nope, it's on your property so it's your responsibility."

Then one phrase hit me. "Wait a minute. *An* electrician? Don't you want this job?"

He closed his notebook and tucked it in his tool bag. "I would love to help you restore this place, Ell. I can see your vision for it. I'd love to be able to put this place on my website as a showcase, but you have some hard decisions to make.

"Like do you want to do it all in one go? Or do you want to make the changes bit by bit? Fix the roof this spring. Redo the kitchen this fall and change out the electrics in the extension at the same time. When does the upstairs ensuite fit in there? At the same time, next year? What are you thinking?"

"Splitting up the kitchen redo and the ensuite might mean I'd live in a middle of a construction zone for years instead of months. And it would mean I'd have to hire you and a plumber to come in twice, right?"

He nodded.

I studied my amended notes. "Do I really need to get quotes from other electricians? I already know I want you to do it. I trust you."

His gaze softened. He lifted his hand and held it over mine as if he wanted to touch me again but pulled it back with a frown. Was I that disgusting that he didn't want to touch me or did he worry he was breaching some business boundary? "Thank you, but you need to know for yourself that I'm giving you the best deal and going to do the best job for you. Plus, it depends on your timeline—I may have already accepted a contract for someone else and won't be able to do the work within your timeframe. So yes, for your own peace of mind, and because I know Joshua will insist anyway, get a couple estimates from other electricians, too."

Hang what Joshua thought. I wanted Malcolm, and not for his electrical knowledge.

Malcolm stood up, grabbed his tool bag and walked to the front door. He stopped on the sidewalk and faced me again. "Oh, and you definitely need to add insulation to the attic. That can save you at least a hundred bucks a month on your heating bill, probably more. I can recommend people you can trust not to hard-sell or upsell you."

Another thing to add to my list. Still, if it saved money in the long run and made me more comfortable. "How long would it take? A complete gut job on the kitchen and all the other stuff. From start to finish?"

"A lot of it depends on supply and demand. Redoing a single house like this, which in most tradesmen's portfolios is a small job, means you'd be lower on their lists for parts and labour. You need to set deadlines with each contractor and get them written into your contracts with whoever you hire. Thing is, Ell, everyone's working on different schedules. So there may be months with nothing happening while you're waiting for someone's schedule to open up. You could have plumbing but no electricity for a week or a month, then you may have electricity but no plumbing because they couldn't get ahold of a specific part because the supply chain was backed up. Lately some items have been unavailable for months. Then there's all the large-scale equipment they'd have to book. Like the septic people need to dig a hole to expand your current system, or your electrician may need to bury the lines from the street, but the backhoe that's needed has been booked out months in advance. In reality, in Port Paxton? You're talking three to six months or possibly longer. It all depends."

He was standing at the base of the stairs, I was one step up, so I could look directly at him. I found myself entranced by his lips, by the way the light spring breeze ruffled his hair. Of the muscles hidden beneath his faded blue brushed-cotton shirt and the way the worn denim clung to his legs, stretched over his groin.

In a move I'd fantasized about since I was a teen, I cupped his cheeks between my palms, leaned in and captured his mouth with mine.

His arms wrapped around me, his fingers digging into

my ass, lifting me to my toes as he kissed me back. I melted against him, his beard scratching my chin, but I didn't care. I loved the feel of his hard chest against mine, the way he groaned into my mouth, making my body soften even more. Then, too soon, he pulled away with a breathed, "Ellie, we shouldn't be doing this."

Had I made a mistake? "Why? We're not in high school anymore."

He brushed a thumb across my cheek. "No, but I shouldn't be kissing you."

"Why not?" I asked, resting my head on his chest. Inhaling him. "Neither of us are dating anyone else." I stiffened. Had Josh or my mom failed to keep me in the loop about that important fact? "Or are you?"

His eyes opened and his gaze skated over my face, my hair, my body. I stopped myself from cringing, expecting some nasty quip about my weight, about my muffin top spilling over my waist band. Or maybe he didn't like the color of my lipstick or—

He shook his head. "No. I'm not dating anyone. But for now? You're a client and I'm trying to maintain a professional distance."

"Stop trying," I whispered.

As he had in all my high school fantasies, he wrapped his arms around me again and lowered his head, resting his forehead against mine. "Do you know how much I've wanted to kiss you again?"

"Why didn't you? Why did you walk away from me in high school? I thought..." He'd asked me to be his date at the prom. Or for my prom. "Or was that kiss a dare or something?"

He grimaced, dropped his hands and stepped away from me again. "I wanted to ask you to the prom but when I mentioned my plans, Josh made me promise to leave you alone, upon pain of death."

I closed my mouth which had apparently dropped open. "Seriously?"

"Yup. That's why I had to walk away." He blanched and ran a hand over his beard. "He's gonna freak if you tell him I broke our pact."

After Dad had left us and moved away, Josh had become overprotective, but he'd seriously enforced a bro code promise on Mal about me? "Kissing me is not a frickin' crime. And you don't have to *admit* anything to Josh. It's none of his business. Besides, I kissed you first, remember?"

He freed a strand of hair caught in my glasses and tucked it behind my ear. "I could have stopped you."

I narrowed my eyes at him. "If you plan on walking away from me now because of some promise you made years ago, you'll have a lot more to deal with than my brother's wrath. You'll have mine. Besides, all we did was kiss, not get into each other's pants."

I couldn't help myself from checking out his jeans and the erection tenting them. Because now I really wanted to check out that bad boy.

"I can't say I didn't enjoy kissing you. Or that I don't want to kiss you again, but..." He shook his head. "You're still mourning. I don't want you to think later that I took advantage of you."

I stood, open-mouthed, as he turned around and walked away. Just like last time.

CHAPTER SIX

MALCOLM

I hadn't expected Ellie to kiss me when I'd rung her doorbell that morning. But once her lips had touched mine and her body melted against me? I couldn't pull away. It was like something that had died within me after Natalie left reignited. I'd wanted to carry her upstairs to her room and strip her naked, to fall onto her bed and explore every part of her body.

But then my promise to Josh hammered at me, as did a small part of my brain wondering if I would be a rebound affair? Is that what they were called for a widow's first journey back into the dating world?

By the time I arrived back at my workshop, I'd convinced myself I was reading too much into it. It was a kiss, nothing more. It was Ellie experimenting with her newfound availability, maybe even from desperation because she was lonely.

Had I kissed her to convince myself that the spark of

attraction I had for her wouldn't ignite into a flame? Or because I hoped it would?

Shit, would Ellie be *my* rebound?

THE NEXT MORNING, I WAS IN THE MIDDLE OF writing up a list of supplies I needed when my security camera app on my phone alerted me that I had a visitor pulling into my driveway. I checked it and recognized my dad's battered old half ton instead of Ellie's sleek SUV. Why was I disappointed that my visitor wasn't Ellie? Why would she come over here anyway?

I unlocked the door and grinned as my father lumbered up to me. "Hey, Dad, what're you doin' in this part of town?"

"Do I need a reason to visit my favourite son?"

I'm his only son, but I still liked him using that line. "No, but usually you get Mom to phone me if you need something." In my entire life, I'd never known Dad to initiate a phone call. I'm not sure if it's a hatred of the technology or if he doesn't like talking over devices rather than a face-to-face interaction, but if a phone call had to be made, he left it to Mom.

He shrugged and made a noncommittal sound as he followed me into my kitchen. We chatted about my business, which was doing well, and about his garden— since he'd retired, Dad spent his days for half the year tending a prize-winning vegetable patch. "I was thinking of putting in a greenhouse this summer. I'd like to run electricity out to it for a fan in the hot days and a heater through the winter. Could you do that for me?"

Mr. Farquharson had only mentioned giving moms free electrical work but I'd extended it to include Dad, too. "Sure. Do you know where you want it?"

After we discussed what size greenhouse he wanted, and the best placement based both on where it would get the most sun and where I'd have to run the electrical lines, he glanced down at Ellie's quote.

"I heard she'd moved back to town," he said with a frown.

"Yup." I flipped the notepad closed. While I'd promised her I wouldn't talk to Josh about her plans for the update, Dad was under no such obligation.

His frown deepened. "You planning on asking her out?"

"No." Geez, I whined like teenager, then cleared my throat and donned my business voice. "I gave her a quote for fixing an electrical issue. I didn't ask her for a date." *Yet.* But I couldn't deny I was definitely wondering how long I'd have to wait to ask her out and how I could convince Josh to forget my damned promise.

Dad raised a graying eyebrow. "Your mother and I could tell you were both eyeing each other in high school. Isn't that why her brother made you promise to leave her alone?"

I could feel the blood rush into my cheeks. "You knew about that?"

"Chantel found out about it when she asked Josh to take her to the prom. He said he wasn't allowed to go out with her any more than you were allowed to go out with his sister."

Even now, my older sister Chantel referred to Josh as GingerNuts with the occasional Satan's Stepchild thrown in, and treated him like an annoying little brother. So why had she asked him to the prom? More importantly, why hadn't either of them told me?

"You had a crush on her. Don't try to deny it. We could all see it," Dad continued as if dismissing my attempt to distract him. "And you definitely were protective of her. Don't you remember when she was being hassled at the town fair that summer before you graduated? How you stepped in and made that guy—what was his name?—back off?"

"Jerry McDonald," I supplied automatically.

One of Dad's eyebrows hitched up and his lips quirked into a smile too. "Interesting how quickly you came up with his name."

"He was a douche." He'd hassled Ellie before the fair that whole year but kept his distance once I'd stepped in, then he'd moved away after high school so he wasn't a problem anymore. I shook it off. "Ellie's still getting her feet under her. I don't think I should be making any moves on her for a while. She's probably not ready." Except for that kiss.

Dad hitched one hip on the edge of my counter and stared past me, his lips pursing in a way that I'd always interpreted as his *I need to word this right look or sparks are going to fly* look. "Your mother and I like Ellie. She's good people. She'd be good for you, and you'd be good for her."

"I made a promise, remember? You always told me that a man's word was worth nothing if he broke it."

"It was a promise you made in high school. And I think Ellie has more say in who she dates, and might take exception to her brother's interference. If he causes problems, your mother or I can say something to Maureen" —Ellie's and Josh's mother—"if you want."

I stopped myself from cringing. That was definitely not a conversation I wanted my father to have in my defense.

"Is that really why you didn't ask Ellie to the prom senior year?" he continued.

I nodded.

"You could have asked her to her prom senior year."

I shook my head. "That was the year the school said only students could be invited, remember? That no outsiders could be attend?" Even though I was a former student, I was one of those who would not be allowed entrance. That unpopular opinion had caused quite an uproar in my old high school, enough that the principal had been replaced the next year. "Then Ellie moved to Kingston for university and I was apprenticing here."

He nodded thoughtfully. "And by the time she'd graduated, you'd moved in with Natalie."

Nat and I had lasted six years before she'd taken a job in Calgary and left me. By then Ellie was married to Hauser. "So?"

Dad drummed his fingers on my desk, stared at something on the far wall and took a deep breath before looking at me again. "We liked Natalie. Don't get me wrong. She was a nice girl. But we never got the feeling either of you were all-in in that relationship. In fact, your mother figures you two lasted three years longer than you should have."

"What the freak, Dad!" I jumped to my feet. "I loved Natalie. I wouldn't have moved in with her if I thought we'd fail."

They say hindsight is twenty-twenty and all that, and only after I looked back on our relationship did I realize the signs that we'd fail had been there from the start. Natalie had wanted to live in a city that didn't fall asleep for six months of the year, a city that had more restaurant and theatre choices. To her, anywhere was more exciting than Port Paxton. Even before we'd moved in together, she'd begged me to move to Toronto and finish my apprenticeship there. But I love living in a village that comes to life every spring as the tourists descend upon us, then returns to its slower pace once the leaves fall and the locals are left to their interests. A town where my family still lives, my friends ...well, some of them were still nearby. Plus, I didn't want to end up working for a larger company, in a city where the average blue-collar worker couldn't afford to buy a house anymore.

It had taken us too long to admit neither of us was happy with the status quo before Natalie had moved out, moved on. Leaving me to feel like I'd let everyone down, not just Natalie, and myself but my family, too. "We're not all destined to be with the same person our entire lives, like you and Mom."

"Hear me out." My dad is the calmest guy I've ever met. But this was the dad giving me his *I'm your dad and I need you to listen because I love you and want the best for you* tone, one I'd long ago learned to listen to. "I'm not saying you didn't treat Natalie right. I think you *think* you loved her, and she thought she loved you. Or at least you both convinced yourselves you did." He tapped my notebook. "But I find it interesting that the very first week Ellie's returned, she's already contacted you."

"I'm an electrician, Dad," I said dryly. "When she had an electrical problem, she phoned the only electrician she knows. That's all that's happening here."

Except for that kiss. Damn it, why did I keep coming back to that?

"Maybe. Maybe not." Dad stood with the old man groan he'd started to make the last few years. "What I'm saying, son, is if your mother's right and you're still carrying a torch for Ellie, go after her. Find out now if she's the one for you. Don't let her slip through your fingers this time."

I found myself staring at my notebook long after he'd left. There were other electricians Ellie could have called. As a one-man outfit, Walsh Electrical isn't at the top of the list when you search for an electrician, alphabetically or otherwise. So how had she gotten my number if she hadn't kept track of me over the years? Joshua hadn't known she'd had an electrical issue until I phoned him, so he hadn't given Ellie my number that morning. So why had Ellie phoned me?

Like my father, I found that interesting.

If I did get together with Ellie, long term or short, I'd lose Josh's friendship, but I hated that walking away from Ellie would cost me a possible future with her. Dad was right. Even if we didn't have a future, didn't we owe it to ourselves to find out?

If Ellie and I took this to the next level, metaphorically

and literally, I had no doubt I'd fall in love with her. Again. But would she fall in love with me or would she use me for sex and then dispose of me like a smelly work sock with a hole in the heel?

I'd already endured that once and didn't want to go through that hell again.

CHAPTER SEVEN

ELLIE

"**E**verything's fine, Josh," I assured my brother. "Mal repaired the outlet and checked the others, too. He also gave me a list of tradespeople he recommends, and another list of people he doesn't recommend. I've got a roofer coming over later this afternoon to give me a quote, and another one promised me he'll come out tomorrow."

Oops, maybe I shouldn't have mentioned Malcolm by name? I still couldn't get over the idea that my own brother had made his best friend swear to never ask me out. Or that Malcolm had agreed, or that all these years later he still worried about Josh's reaction.

"Whatever you do, don't take the first quote they offer. And research the companies and look at the ratings, good *and* bad," my brother said.

"Josh, I've done my research, okay?" His obvious advice frustrated me but life with Gareth had taught to keep my tone level, unreadable.

How different would my life have been if Josh hadn't made Malcolm swear to walk away from me? Would we have survived as a couple while I went to college? Or would we have split up, like he had with his girlfriend Natalie? Why *had* he split up with Natalie?

My mother, who is good friends with Malcolm's mom Louise, had kept me in the loop about Malcolm, though I was never sure if she realized that my questions about him were not completely innocent.

"Maybe I should come over," Josh fretted. "They might be more honest with a guy around."

Good thing we weren't on a video call because my eyes were rolling so hard, he wouldn't have missed it. The worst part was admitting he was probably right. "You can't leave the office in the middle of tax season. I know how swamped you are, and Mom wouldn't be happy with you leaving her in the lurch."

He *hmm*ed in agreement. "I worry about you, Ell. I don't want to see you taken advantage of. I'm trying to help."

Except his *help* had interfered with a potential relationship with Malcolm back in high school.

"Josh?" I asked, hating the hesitation in my voice. "Why did you make Mal swear not to ask me out back in high school? Is there something wrong about him that you've never told me?"

A gusty sigh preceded his, "He told you about that, huh?"

"Yes. So why did you warn him away?"

"Because he was my best friend and you were my little sister. If something happened between you, if you two didn't work out, I was afraid I'd have to choose and I'd always choose you, Ell."

"So you interfered because you thought you might lose him as a friend if we broke up?"

"In case you don't remember, I wasn't exactly the most popular kid back in high school."

No, with his then-thick glasses, curly red hair and slight belly that these days would be called a dad bod, plus Josh's affinity for math and puzzles, he hadn't been one of the cool kids. I hadn't realized how much it affected him. Maybe because I hadn't been one of the cool kids either?

"If it makes you feel any better, I had to promise to stay away from Chantel," he said dryly.

"You don't even like Chantel. You two were always at each other's throats." Still were.

"I know, but he said if he had to stay clear of my sister, I had to stay clear of his."

I shook my head to clear it and forced myself back on track. "So he doesn't have a bad temper or anything?"

"No, Ell. Mal's one of the good guys. He doesn't yell when he gets angry. He gets quieter."

"You mean like he gives you the silent treatment?" Gareth had done that a lot and I'd grown to hate it.

"No. He gets even more patient. I don't know how he does it, but he's the most freaking reasonable guy under pressure I've met. His dad is the same, don't you remember?"

Okay, that was good. "D'you know why he and Natalie broke up?"

A long pause. "You'd have to ask him. Are you really interested in him still?"

"Yes." I stopped myself from blurting, *I kissed him yesterday. And I liked it.* Nor did I admit that I wanted to do a hell of a lot more than kiss Malcolm. Neither confession would would go over well with my brother. "I want to ask him out, but I don't want you interfering again, okay? Promise me?"

There was a long pause because Josh replied, "Are you sure you're ready for a relationship? That you're done grieving Gareth?"

Gareth's death had been a relief, but the only people I'd admitted that to so far were my therapist and my mom. The latter of whom may have told Josh but I wasn't sure. "He's been dead nearly two years. And I have been on a couple dates already." Disasters both but I wasn't about to admit that.

"Are you sure about this?" Josh asked.

Josh is not Gareth. He's not controlling you, I repeated to myself when I found it hard to breathe. Josh was simply trying to look out for me like he had all my life, like a big brother should. "No. But it's Malcolm. Not a stranger who would be even more of a risk. I've known him all my life. You're his best friend. Doesn't that give him a seal of approval?"

Not that Josh's approval mattered to me. He'd liked Gareth. Everybody had liked Gareth. Only I saw what he was really like behind closed doors. Well, maybe his lovers on the side had an inkling, not that it stopped them from sleeping with my husband.

Josh blew out a breath and I could picture him running his hands through his hair, making it stick up in all directions. "All right. I'll try not to interfere. But if

Malcolm hurts you, I'm going to pound his face in, you hear me?"

Which was as good as I'd get, I decided.

Two hours after I'd hung up on Josh, and after I'd finished a video call with a client, I found myself wandering around the house, returning again and again to stare at the kitchen outlet that had brought Malcolm back into my life. I was standing there, remembering the kiss I'd given him, the way he'd responded, when the doorbell rang.

I opened the door, expecting to find the roofer. Instead, Malcolm stared back at me, wearing another set of workpants liberally spattered with something that looked like drywall spackle, and a black t-shirt that said "Electricians Do It in the Dark." He also had a peace lily tucked under one arm.

"What are you doing here?" I blurted out, then realized it sounded rude. "Is there something wrong? Do you need an answer about your quote already?"

CHAPTER EIGHT

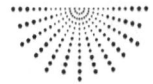

MALCOLM

I opened my mouth to answer her, but my tongue got all tangled up on an answer. She was in a different outfit this afternoon. She'd pulled her hair into some fancy do, had done her makeup so her eyes looked bigger than normal, and wore a white professional-looking button-up blouse with the top two buttons undone, revealing a chunky necklace of some shiny black stone that would be fit for working an office. But from waist down she wore red-and-black plaid pajama-style pants, and those adorable pink bunny slippers.

Maybe she'd been on one of the video conferences where she only had to look businesslike from the waist up?

But the way she stared at me, eyes wide, those lush lips parted, waiting for my response, made me want to kiss her senseless. To take her in my arms, carry her up the stairs, strip us both naked and have wild, uninhibited sex.

"Nope, nothing's wrong." I gestured with my chin toward the front door. "Can I come in?"

She nodded and led the way. I stepped inside, dumped the plant on the side table beside the dish where she kept her keys.

"As for why I'm here, I've been thinking about doing this since last time I saw you."

Then, mirroring what she'd done with me, I took her face in my hands and brushed my lips against hers. She tilted her head and returned the kiss with a moan of desire that made my dick uncomfortably hard. She wrapped her arms around me, her fingers digging into my ass, pulling me closer as she ground against me. A coconut scent wafted off her, and she tasted of it too, though maybe that was her lip gloss? Another quiet sound escaped her, not of pain or complaint, but like a cat's purr.

Without breaking our kiss, I kicked the door closed with my heel. The ticktock of the ancient grandfather clock in the hallway stood as a slow counterpoint to my racing heart.

We were both breathing hard by the time we broke the kiss. It took all my effort not to make good on my fantasy of hauling her upstairs.

To distract myself from my fantasies of stripping her naked and taking her right there on the stairs, I nodded toward the plant I'd brought her. "Mom asked me to give this to you as a housewarming gift," I lied. I'd bought it myself fully intending to use it as an icebreaker, a way to see her again. "It's supposed to help clean the air."

"Thanks." She grabbed the potted plan and placed it on

the mantel in the living room. Then stood there, staring at it.

She finally lifted her eyes to meet mine. Her eyes weren't shiny like she'd been fighting tears, but there was a bruised air about her, like she was haunted. "We need to talk."

Shit. That was exactly what Natalie had said when she'd announced she was leaving me. Even if Ellie was about to say, "I don't want to see you again," at least I'd know there was no future with her.

Bracing for the worst, I nodded. "Okay."

I waited for her to start. Except she didn't. She simply stood there, staring at the floor between us.

"Ell? Do you want me to leave?"

With a shake of her head, she closed her eyes. "No. I'm being stupid, that's all."

What happened to the confident Ellie from high school? "You're the least stupid person I know. So what's going on?"

Another small shake of her head.

"What do we need to talk about?" How could I make this better? What had I done wrong? Shit. She'd kissed me first the other day, but maybe she'd regretted it afterward? "Am I the first guy you've kissed since your husband...?"

Shit! Should I have mentioned him? Or not asked at all? Fuck! I was such an idiot. Now I wanted to bang my head against the wall.

She shook her head without raising it. "No, I've dated a couple times since Gareth..."

From the way she didn't—couldn't?—say died either, I figured she was still grieving and I'd breached her boundaries. I wanted to cuddle her but...boundaries. Last thing I wanted to do was make her feel crowded, make her want to distance herself even more.

"Ell? What can I do to make it better? What do you need?"

She launched herself against me, burying her face against my neck, her whole body taut against mine. What the hell do I do now? How do I fix whatever I've done? I had no idea. So I held her, rubbing her back as she pressed harder against me, her body now shaking. It took me a couple seconds before I realized she wasn't crying but laughing.

"Ell?" I was floundering here, but I didn't know what to do, what to say.

"It's not you. It's me. I told you." She shook her head, then blew out a breath. "Well, in a way it is you, but not in the way you think."

I stayed quiet because the way she worded it sounded like a two-edged sword that could swing back on me pretty damned quick. She finally lifted her head and stepped away to tug me over to the couch. She sat on the cushion beside me, turned sideways so she faced me and hitched one leg beneath her.

"So...that kiss means there's something still between us, right? I mean, I'm not the only one feeling this...attraction, am I? Or...am I?" she asked.

"No. It's still there." I wanted to reach for her, to drag her onto my lap but she was fighting something that I didn't understand, that I knew was important and she needed space.

"Okay, good. I need to tell you something before we take whatever we've got going on any further."

Hope and fear leapt up in me. She wanted to take things further, but it came with a *but* that worried me. "All right."

"I've only told my mom about this," she scrunched up her nose and hugged herself, "and she may have told Josh, but I'd prefer if you don't go talking about this with anyone else. Even your parents. You know how gossip travels in Port Paxton."

Did I ever. "Okay."

"Before he died, things between Gareth and I were...rough. They had been for a while. I realize now, it was always bad and that I should never have married him, but it was only the last few months I finally admitted to myself that I needed to get out. Mainly because of the way he'd been treating me. It took me too long to realize how he'd isolated me from my family, my friends. Then I discovered he'd been cheating on me. Like serial cheating, pretty much our whole marriage. So I hired a lawyer to get my ducks in a row before I told Gareth I was leaving."

Fuck.

"I had everything arranged and planned to tell him I wanted a divorce."

"You'd moved your stuff out?"

Another shake of her head. "No. My lawyer advised me not to move out, that I had the rights to half of the condo. They'd told me a lot more but they said unless I was afraid he'd get physical, to encourage him to move out or move into the second bedroom for one of us until we could work everything out."

There was something about the way she'd mentioned physical abuse that set the hairs on the back of my neck crawling. "Was he? Abusing you?"

"He never hit me," she said so quietly I had to strain to hear her. "But words can hurt as much as fists. And he knew how to use his words to hurt the most. He was really good at manipulating me, at making me doubt myself. I didn't realize how much he'd been gaslighting me until I went into therapy after he died. That's when I started remembering how he'd convinced me that the reason I was so unhappy was because I was always interpreting things incorrectly, that I was weak. That I expected too much, that I wasn't good enough. That I was the reason for anything going wrong." Another deep breath.

"He chose every piece of clothing I was to wear every day. He monitored what I ate, made sure I exercised to his specifications. He'd check my phone to make sure I wasn't talking with people he didn't approve of. He'd monitor my texts. He stopped me...from seeing..." The words seemed to catch in her throat.

"He stopped you from visiting your family," I said softly. I grabbed the box of tissues from the side table and handed it to her.

She nodded as she dabbed the tissue against her eyes. "Sometimes Mom would ask me if everything was okay, but he never let me be alone with her or Josh. He was always right there and I couldn't say anything. After he died, I discovered he'd put tracking software on it so he was getting copies of my texts and everything I sent. Which made me really glad that after I decided to leave him, I'd bought a different phone that he didn't know about, and created new bank accounts and new email accounts."

I wondered if her mother, Maureen, had confided any of this to my mother—they'd been best friends since grade school. If she had, she'd probably sworn my mother to secrecy too. If Mom had promised not to say anything, she wouldn't even tell Dad. Mom was absolutely a deep well when it came to guarding secrets, mine or anyone's.

"I wish I'd known. I would have come down there and gotten you out of there." *Protected you.*

"I probably wouldn't have left. Not for the first few years anyway. He had me so convinced I was the one at fault. That I needed him to keep my life in order."

She dropped her gaze, picking at some fluff on the couch. "I was waiting for him to come home so I could tell him I wanted a divorce, right? Except he didn't come home. Instead, the police knocked on the door and told me he had been in a car accident—that he'd been speeding. It was snowing and the roads were slick. He'd missed a corner, rolled the car and...he was dead."

Divorce bullet dodged, as far as I was concerned, but I wasn't about to say that aloud.

Her voice grew so quiet I had to lean in to hear her, especially since she wouldn't look at me. "Part of me was relieved he was dead. I felt guilty about that for a long time. I felt guiltier when people would come up and tell me they were so sorry about everything, tell me what a nice guy he was. When I wanted to scream that I wasn't sorry. That he was a fucking asshole. But I couldn't, you know?"

"I think that's a reasonable response."

She drew a deep breath and straightened, forcing

strength into her voice. "Anyway, Gareth's gone, and I'm doing really well now."

"Do you have anyone to talk to?"

"You mean like a therapist? Yeah. Rebecca. She's been wonderful from our first session. I'd barely started telling her about Gareth when she'd shaken her head and said, 'Everything he told you? Everything he tried to make your fault? Fuck that shit.' Right then, I knew I'd found the right person. With Rebecca's help, I started regaining my self-confidence."

I brushed the back of my knuckles against her cheek. "I'm glad you found her."

She leaned her cheek against my fingers. "So am I. Though it took me about a year of therapy to finally accept it wasn't my fault. But now? Seeing you? Being around you? I've finally realized what I've been missing all those years."

I pulled her onto my lap and cuddled her, thinking over all she'd told me, wondering how blind Gareth had been to miss what a great person she is, the damage he'd done to her self-image, what might be the best way to approach a relationship with her, and if it was too soon, when I realized she'd fallen asleep.

I stroked her hair, trailed my fingers over her shoulders and down her arm and kissed the top of her head. Was Dad right? Had I unconsciously sabotaged my relationship with Natalie because I was hoping Ellie would return home one day and we'd find each other again?

I wound that question around in my head for too long before deciding we'd both screwed up that relationship and I learned from it. Now I had a fresh start with Ellie.

Ellie, who had trailed around after Josh and me as a toddler, insisting we have tea parties on the lawn where all our friends could see us. Ellie, who on her first day at my high school, had bounded up to me and chattered nonstop, revealing things about me to my friends that I really didn't want them to know. Ellie, who treated everyone like they were her best friend, whether they were the janitor, the cafeteria ladies, or the prissy cheerleaders who mocked her to her face.

Ellie, who loved this house and trusted me with her vision to restore it. Who, after years of living with an asshole, trusted me by telling me something she'd never shared outside of her family.

That was huge.

I needed to research what might trigger her, what to do if I triggered her accidentally, how not to trigger her. There was so much to research. But I knew I wanted to be there for her. I didn't want this to be a one-time thing. I wanted her in my life, lying here beside me with those silly bunny slippers staring up at me, though hopefully from the floor, for the rest of my life.

But was she ready for a long-term relationship? Was I, or would I screw it up the way I had with Natalie?

My balls shrank at the thought that Ellie might suggest we make this a friends-with-benefits relationship. Or worse, a one-night stand. They got harder at the idea she might then go out and fall in love with someone else, expecting me to stand by with my thumb up my ass, wishing her the best.

"You're thinking awful hard." Her voice broke the silence. "Want to share?" She pulled back and stared at me, her head tilted to one side. "No, let me guess. You're trying to figure out if I'm ready to be in a relationship."

I nodded, unable to verbally respond. The idea of her dating other men bugged the shit out of me.

"I've dated a few times already. But none of them were...right. Anyway, this—" she circled her finger between us "—you and me? You're...different. I can't explain it."

She bit her bottom lip, as if she were doing a mental play-by-play of how I'd kissed her. Talk about a fast way to shrivel my 'nads.

"You...care." She nodded as if more confident in her choice. "Yeah, that's it. You're focused on me. I'm not used to that."

"Then any guy you've been with is an asshat."

She wiggled off my lap and sat beside me once more, pulling her legs to her chest and hugging them. "I've talked with Rebecca about that a lot lately. She thinks I am ready. So, the way I see it, we have three choices. The first is we have a one-and-done sex session and we walk away and never speak of it again." She held up her hand with one finger extended, watching me closely. When I didn't respond, she said, "I don't like that choice."

Thank God. "Me either."

She touched her thumb to her middle finger. "Two, the friends-with-benefits option." She pursed her lips and shook her head. "Nope, not liking that option either."

Her thumb moved to her ring finger. "We keep seeing each other and see where this goes from there."

"I like that idea." Though I still had to deal with Josh and my broken promise.

She nodded and lowered her hands, staring at them. "I

know it's early days yet, but if we do this, if we see each other, you don't see anyone else."

I didn't want to date anyone else, and I didn't want to see her on the arm of someone else wandering around town or sitting across from another man at the Pancake Shack or one of the local restaurants. "I can agree to that. So do you want to tell Josh or should I?"

She huffed out a breath and crossed her arms over her chest, mashing her breasts into a delightful mound I wanted to play with. "I'm really pissed at Josh for making you promise to back off back in high school. If I'd been dating you…" Her voice broke but I could hear her unvoiced *I wouldn't have ended up with Gareth.*

Which we both knew wasn't necessarily true.

"Hindsight's twenty-twenty. You can't play that type of coulda-woulda-shoulda mind game with yourself. You can't change the past."

She blew out another long breath and shook her head. "Yeah, Rebecca says that too. I'll tell him when we're at Mom's for Sunday dinner. Mom'll back me up and make sure he understands he's got no say in who I date."

"All right. But if you need me, text me and I'll be there, all right?"

"Thank you, I know I can trust you," she said, her confidence in me strong in her tone.

Except I'd broken my promise to Josh, hadn't I?

CHAPTER NINE

ELLIE

Malcolm stuck around until the roofer came, giving me the same reason that Josh had done. The roofer might give me a better deal with a guy keeping an eye on him. Especially since he knew Mal.

Once the roofer pulled out of the driveway, Mal turned to me. "I gotta get going, too." He tilted his head. "D'you want to go out tomorrow? Maybe drive to Peterborough? Play tourist, then have dinner?"

"Like an actual date?"

He nodded. "Like an actual date. Though you don't need to worry about doing the whole hair and makeup routine. Unless you want to."

"You're supposed to say I don't need makeup, that I'm beautiful just the way I am."

He barked a laugh and wrapped his arms around me until I rested against him. "Well, that's true. Or we could rent a boat and go over to the sandbar and swim, then do dinner here."

"I haven't gone swimming in ages but it's too early in the year. The water's still freezing. As for dinner here, you'd have to promise your idea of dinner isn't ordering a burger at Pinpals." Port Paxton's five-pin bowling alley.

Was that a hint of a blush on his cheeks?

I shut my mouth which had dropped open. "Wait a minute. Don't tell me you actually did that to Natalie or one of your other dates?"

He shrugged, but his blush deepened. "Not Natalie. A girl from Toronto who was staying at her parents' cottage and was bored."

"When was this?" Please tell me it wasn't recently.

"The summer I got my first job apprenticing. I was young and broke and I thought combining dinner with bowling sounded like fun."

I laughed at his sheepish expression. "Lesson learned then." I thought about his suggestions. "Wandering around Peterborough sounds fun. I haven't been there in ages."

"Good. I'll pick you up around eleven?"

"Sounds like a plan." A plan to keep us out of Josh's line of sight until I had a chance to talk to him about Malcolm and I dating. I leaned up on my toes and kissed Malcolm's neck, nuzzling his beard. I know a lot of women prefer clean-shaven guys, but I liked the way his beard scratched against my skin. "So where are you off to now?"

"I have a quote of my own to give to a client in..." He checked his watch and swore. "Thirty minutes and it'll take me thirty-five to get there unless I break the speed limit."

"Then go." I stepped away from him and pushed his chest. "You mustn't keep your client waiting."

He gave me a hard lingering kiss, then grabbed his jacket and raced out of the house, the screen door banging behind him, calling, "See you tomorrow."

I gave him a thumbs-up sign as he put his truck in gear and tore out of my driveway. Here's hoping he remembered the speed trap down by Foster's Glen and didn't get a ticket.

Considering I'd accepted a date the first week I'd returned to Port Paxton, was *I* moving too fast? Nah. This was Malcolm, and dating him was a long time coming.

MALCOLM WAS LATE THAT SATURDAY. ONLY BY five minutes, but I'd half convinced myself I was being stood up. Then my phone dinged that a text message from Malcolm had arrived. Fuck.

I drew a deep breath, steeling myself for that "Sorry, I have to cancel" message. Instead, I read,

MALCOLM

"Sorry, running late. Be there in ten."

When the doorbell rang minutes fourteen minutes later, the memory of answering the door and finding the police on the other side, wearing grim expressions, flooded back. My mouth dry, I opened the door to find Malcolm standing on my porch, his expression sheepish.

"I'm sorry, Ell. I didn't think it would take me so long to walk here."

Walk? Only then did I realize his truck wasn't in the driveway.

"My truck is havin'...issues so I don't trust it not to leave us stranded. We can hang around here, maybe order a pizza or some Chinese food from that new place that's just opened?" His voice changed, grew less confident. "I'd totally understand if you want to cancel."

Wow, he was expecting me to cancel because his truck broke down? Did women actually do that?

"I can drive us to Peterborough." I mockingly narrowed my eyes at him. "Or are you one of those cavemen who insist that only men are capable of driving?"

I wasn't sure if I was joking or not. But Malcolm readily agreed. As I pulled out of the driveway with Malcolm riding shotgun, I found myself surprised that he'd capitulated such control to me. Even since our first date, Gareth had demanded to drive every time. We *always* took his car, and he *always* drove. But Malcolm had settled into the passenger seat and made himself comfortable.

Driving to Peterborough took us along a winding two-lane highway, along the shore of Hawkeshead Lake, where we discussed how they had finally tamed the washboard effect over the causeway. With the lake behind us, we discussed the problems with his truck, and the difficulty of being self-employed and having to deal with unreasonable clients. The whole time, I was aware of Malcolm's sitting beside me. He didn't once clutch the door handle or hiss as I threaded through the early arrivals of traffic on Port Paxton's streets or dealt with impatient tourists on the highway passing me on the double line so they could get to their cottages five minutes ahead of the next guy. With his casual manner and easy conversation, I found myself gradually relaxing.

As I slowed to drive through a pretty little village a tenth the size of Port Paxton, I gestured with my head to Ski Hill Road. "Do you still ski?"

He shook his head. "Not much now they've closed down both the lodges. I mean I could go to the hill in Kirby, or the one south of Uxbridge, but..."

"But you're afraid you'll break your leg again?" I teased. Malcolm had twice broken his leg—technically, he'd broken each leg once.

He snorted. "No. And I only broke my left leg because Gary Olsen cut right in front of me. He never should have been on that hill—it was way above his skill level."

In that incident, Gary had ended up with a broken arm as well as a concussion, and blamed Malcolm for it still. But Malcolm was right. Gary had only started skiing that year and shouldn't have been on the advanced slope.

As we approached the edge of Peterborough, we decided neither of us were hungry yet so I drove to the lift locks first. I'd been there once, as part of a school trip, and been bored silly at the time, but this time, walking along the river at the base of the lock, I found it pretty. Restful. Or maybe that was because I was with Malcolm.

We stopped to watch along the canal's edge as, what the sign describing the giant rectangular water-filled bathtub called a caisson, slowly lowered two kayaks, a houseboat and a couple cabin cruisers—one twenty-footer and one closer to thirty feet with a pilothouse and flying bridge—sixty-five feet to continue their trek along the Trent River.

As we watched, Malcom's hand touched mine, and our

fingers entwined. The calluses on his palms showed a man who was not afraid of hard work, yet his touch was gentle. Warm. Comforting. Why did my heart rate jump? I had been married, was a widow before I turned forty. Yet here I was, grinning to myself that we were holding hands, as if I were still a teenager.

Aware of his shoulder brushing against mine, I asked, "Have you ever taken your boat through the lift locks?"

His parents had a small motor boat that his father used for fishing rather than cruising. "Nah. I've taken our boat through the locks at Fenelon Falls and Bobcaygeon, but it would take all day to get from Port Paxton to here and back again. Might be fun to do if I had a cabin cruiser or a houseboat and wanted to travel the entire length of the Trent."

As the gates pivoted down, allowing the boats out of the caisson, and they began to manoeuvre their way past us, two buses sporting a church group banner pulled into the parking lot. They unloaded a mixture of seniors who slowly ambled along the walk, and younger families with school-aged kids who raced along the path toward us, hooting and hollering despite their parents' admonitions.

The peace of the park broken, we decided to leave. It took us less than ten minutes to head back downtown. Peterborough's one-way main streets, both of which followed the path of the Trent River, always confused me, even with the GPS. Which had sometimes steered me to drive down the main street the wrong way. With Malcolm beside me, keeping an eye out for street signs, I safely eased into the parkade and parked it on the second story. Malcolm hopped out and rounded my car as I did the same.

He held out his hand and once again I placed my palm in his. We wandered along George, then back along Water St.

Malcolm didn't complain when I tugged into one of the used bookstores. Nor did he grumble about the time I took to peruse the stacks. At some point I realized he'd wandered away but I found him in the mystery section checking out an older Louise Penny novel. By the time we stepped out of the store, we each had a bulging bag, mine containing an eclectic collection of mysteries, romances and several books for beginner gardeners. His contained several books, the one by Louise, as well as older titles by Linwood Barclay, Thomas King, and a battered copy of the history of Rome.

Even though it was still mid-afternoon, we agreed we were both hungry and we could avoid the dinner crowds if we ate now, so we headed to the restaurant we'd decided upon earlier. I ordered a poached pear salad while Malcolm ordered the pulled pork poutine and one of their craft beers, along with a spinach-and-cheese dip as an appetizer.

We picked at the appetizer as we discussed our reading preferences, about changes I wanted to make to the house that wouldn't involve the electrical or plumbing, and he grossed me with tales of stuff he'd discovered in walls or attics as part of his job. I hadn't laughed so much or been so relaxed and had such an enjoyable conversation in years.

He actually listened to what I said and asked questions without making me feel stupid. When the waitress brought him the wrong poutine, he politely pointed out the mistake. Where Gareth would have made a scene, demanded to see the manager to have our food comped, Malcolm waved off her apologies and told her how he'd worked at the Pancake Shack and knew what it was like dealing with the public.

Stop it! Stop comparing him to Gareth. See Malcolm for Malcolm. Appreciate him for who he is, not how different he is from your dead husband. Gareth is dead, gone. He's not your problem anymore. Don't let that asshole keep occupying your thoughts, commanding space in your brain.

"What?" Malcolm had put down his fork and tilted his head in question.

I stared at him in confusion. "What what?"

"You blanked out for a bit there. I was talking but it was like I was talking to a statue."

Shit. "I'm sorry. I got lost in some thoughts."

Another searching look as if he knew I was lying. Which I was, and wasn't. "Want to share? I'm a good listener."

How would I like it if Malcolm told me he was comparing me to his ex? Yeah, no. Not going to happen. With Rebecca, sure, but not Malcolm.

"I was drifting. Sorry."

MALCOLM

I'd caught how Ellie had blushed when I'd held her hand at the lift locks, and again in the parkade, though it had faded as we walked down George St. That time in the restaurant when she'd zoned out had worried me though. She'd tried to wave it off, but something had triggered her. For now, she seemed balanced, and even happy, given the tilt at the corner of her lips.

As we left the restaurant, neither of us was ready to head home yet, so we found ourselves walking along the trail leading to Little Lake. The warmth of the evening enhanced the scent Ellie was wearing, which went straight to my groin. It took all of my willpower not to suggest we go back to the car and neck. Or even better, stop off at the hotel overlooking the lake and rent a room for the night.

She stepped closer to avoid an oncoming bicyclist, bumping her hip against mine. Somehow, I ended up facing her, and without thinking, my arms went around her hips, pulling her against me. Or maybe her arms went around my hips and pulled me close against her. My breath caught as she tilted her head and slanted her lips against mine.

She smelled so good, something flowery and spicy, not overpowering but sexy as fuck. Her breath feathered over my cheek, and the softness of her breasts pressed against my chest, making my dick rock hard and aching against my zipper. Her hands slid from my waist to cup my butt and pull me closer, grinding herself against me with a low moan.

Someone further along the path yelled, "Get a room, you two," and we broke apart, both breathing heavily. Ellie's blush returned and she looked adorable. Until her gaze skittered across the lake.

I cupped my fingers beneath her chin. "Hey, we're both consenting adults. There's no need to be embarrassed. We were kissing, that's all."

She huffed a laugh. "I know, but still, I feel like I'm back at uni."

I raised my eyebrows. "You've had that yelled at you before?"

A reluctant nod but her gaze still wouldn't meet mine. "I told you I went a little wild when I moved down to Kingston. Especially the first year." She grimaced. "I nearly failed because I'd turned into a party girl until Mom threatened to stop paying my room and board."

Huh. Did I really want to know this? "I've heard university life can be..."

"Wild? A sex-fest?" she supplied with a broad smile. "Hedonistic?"

"Maturing," I finished.

"Maturing," she repeated. "I prefer that choice." Her gaze finally slid toward me, then skittered down to my chin. "So d'you want to go back to my place? Or yours?"

My chubby that had been deflating after the catcall perked up again at her suggestion.

"Mine?" I'd cleaned my place this morning, on a very hopeful chance we ended up there. Okay, I'd cleaned the living room, kitchen, bathroom and my bedroom. The other rooms? I'd keep the doors shut until I could do a better clean. I also wouldn't mention that I'd checked the expiration date on my stash of condoms—can't be too careful about that shit. I'd even stuck two spares in my wallet, in case she invited me in to her place. But it was our first date, so I figured they'd stay where they were. As long as Josh didn't drive by my place and see Ellie's SUV parked outside in the morning. Luckily, I lived down a sideroad he wouldn't have any reason to take.

The moon glittered over the lake as we drove back into Port Paxton, a light breeze wafting the scent of my neighbour's lilacs across the lawn when Ellie pulled into my place. I glanced at her and found her watching me out the corner of her eye, her bottom lip caught between her teeth. "I'm not expecting anything. If you want to talk, and not take it any further, I'm good with that."

Her gaze flickered to my door, illuminated by the light I'd left on, the occasional moth batting against it. "I think we're past talking, aren't we?"

CHAPTER TEN

ELLIE

I wanted this. I wanted Malcolm. The entire drive back to Port Paxton I'd been mulling over different things I wanted to do to him. With him. Should I do a slow striptease to build the heat between us? Or should I give in to my impulse to strip his clothes off him, push him down on his couch, or preferably his bed, and ride him until we both lost our minds? I'd even eyed the pull off overlooking the lake that was often used as a make-out spot and wondered if we should just get down and dirty like we were two teens. Except there were already two cars parked at either end and I really wasn't interested in worrying about the stick shift, or an audience.

Yet once we'd pulled into his driveway, he'd offered me an out. Had he changed his mind about wanting to have sex with me?

Then I noticed the bulge in his crotch and my lips slowly tugged into a smile. Nah, he wanted me too. I leaned over and kissed him, the console digging into my ribs and making me glad I hadn't pulled into what the locals referred to as Make-Out Point. Consoles and stick shifts made making out that much more difficult to coordinate. Not impossible, but more of a challenge than necessary considering there was a bed waiting for us beyond that battered green wooden door.

The moment my lips touched his, he moaned and cupped his hand at the back of my head, holding me as he took over the kiss. He smelled so good, kissed even better, a skill he'd perfected since that brief stolen kiss back in high school. I squelched the question of who had helped him practice. I'd had my own share of practice partners, too. By the time his hold loosened and I leaned back, we were both panting like racehorses.

"No. I haven't changed my mind," I assured him, though I was pretty sure he'd already figured that out. I removed the keys from the ignition, opened my door and headed up his driveway, leaving him to follow.

By the time I reached his front door, he was right behind me, his keys in hand. He wrapped a hand around my waist, reached around me and unlocked his door. Once inside, he kicked the door closed, turned the deadbolt and faced me, the heat in his gaze searing me, as if it could melt my clothes from me. Yet he said not a word.

I dropped my purse on the floor at my feet and stalked toward him, closing the distance between us like a cat advancing on its prey. Not dropping my gaze, I reached up and found the top button of his shirt and flicked it loose. Then the second button, and the third.

He swallowed hard, but didn't stop me. Not that I

wanted to be stopped. By the time I had freed all the buttons, I spread the two sides of his shirt wide and splayed my fingers over his chest. His breath hitched at my touch but I loved that he let me take charge like this. Let me explore his body at my leisure.

Years of manual labour had defined his physique, his pecs hard beneath my fingertips and his skin warm. His breath hitched again as I lowered my palms, skimmed them over his belly, and found the tops of his jeans. Undid the button at his fly, and lowered the zipper.

Only then did I drop my gaze to his cock straining against the confines of his black—or maybe it was dark blue, we hadn't turned on the lights yet—underwear. A quick tug, and a push of both his underwear and jeans to his knees, I freed his cock, its rigid length making my body soften at the promise of him inside me, taking me, pleasuring me.

Still, he stood there, his gaze intense as he said nothing, made no demands, gave no commands.

I raised my gaze and met his again as I slowly lowered myself to my knees. He hissed in a breath as I ran my tongue around his swollen head. I played with him, both with my tongue and by wrapping my hand around his hard shaft, testing to see what made him react, made his breath stop, his body shudder. Without warning, I took his length in my mouth, and earned a rough "Holy fuck" that echoed throughout the room. As I sucked him deeply, until the tip of his cock touched the back of my throat, I rolled his globes in one palm, loving his groans and the way his body tightened and twitched at each touch, each increase and release of suction.

My own hips were rolling with the motion, pressing my clit against my heel until I was ready to come, when his hands clamped around my head and stopped me.

"Enough." His voice was rough.

Oh shit, was he one of those one-and-done type guys?

His lips curved into a smile as if he sensed my concern. "I don't want to come in your mouth. Not yet. I want to be buried deep inside your sweet little pussy that first time. I want to feel you come around me first."

Oh fuck. I'd had guys talk dirty to me, but there was something about Malcolm, his tone, his promise, I don't know which but my pussy dampened my panties and my body quivered in need at his confession, his promise.

He lifted me to my feet and kicked off his jeans, his cock sticking out proudly as he led me down the unlit hall and opened another door, revealing his bedroom. Before I cleared the threshold, he pressed me against the door frame, capturing my mouth, while his hands lifted my skirt and tugged my panties down past my knees. He tapped my feet until I moved them farther apart.

Then he announced, "My turn," and lowered himself to his knees in front of me.

I swallowed my laugh when his head disappeared beneath the fabric but the laugh changed to a whimper of need when his hot breath followed by an even hotter tongue swipe across my clit, licking, stabbing across my sensitive bud. His fingers soon followed, penetrating me, giving me more pleasure with tongue and fingers than I'd had in... ever. The man proved he knew female anatomy as he pleasured me until my whole body shook and my legs could barely support me.

I wanted—needed—to take this action to the bed, to have him on top of me, filling me with his cock instead of his fingers but I couldn't speak, couldn't ask, didn't want to ask because I didn't want to stop whatever it was he was doing. He did something, hit a spot that made me come harder than I ever had before. My whole body seized with the pleasure he teased from me, and I couldn't stop the orgasm that lasted longer and was harder than any I could remember. And he'd done it simply with his tongue and fingers. What would it be like with him inside me?

Before I could collapse onto the floor, he lifted me in his arms and carried me to the bed.

"Fuck me, Mal. Please?" I'd wanted to come across as sexy, as in control, but I heard the need in my voice and wondered if he'd hear it as a weakness. But at this point I didn't care. The tremor of my orgasm still quivered as I shucked off my clothes and stretched out on his mattress. "I need you inside me. Fuck me and fuck me hard."

MALCOLM

After Ell had told me about her treatment under her husband's hand, I figured I'd need to take things slow, to treat her gently. To let her take the lead. I'd planned to lie on the bed and have her ride me, leave her completely in control so as to not trigger her in any way.

When she'd gone down on her knees in the hallway, I'd been shocked both at her gesture and at the skill she had that made me damned near come too fast. Now she was splayed out, completely naked on my bed, a confident sex goddess knowing exactly she wanted, what she needed. Demanding I pleasure her.

Fuck yeah, I was down for that. I stripped off my shirt, the only remaining garment I wore, tossed it on the floor behind me. I opened the bedside table and found the box of condoms I'd stashed there, grabbed one and rolled it on. Not wasting a second, I mounted the bed, straddling her hips, my cock bumping against her mound.

I bent down to capture one of her nipples between my teeth, needing to taste them, to play with them—she'd always had great tits, perky things that I'd fantasized about senior year.

"Yeah, yeah, suck on them all you want while you're fucking me," she huffed in exasperation, lifting her hips and rolling them against my cock in an implicit demand.

Gorgeous woman beneath me demanding I fuck her hard? Yeah, talk about a total fantasy moment. Who was I to deny such a request?

Even in the dark of the room, her pussy glistened, telling me she was wet and ready for me. I positioned the head of my cock at her entrance, and swiped my thumb over her clit. Her whole body jerked in response, her hips arched even more, pressing my dick halfway down her passage. Oh fuck, she was tight, pulsing around my shaft like a throbbing glove.

Her moan, one of pleasure, resonated in my chest. Despite her entreaties to take her fast and hard, I prolonged both our pleasure, my thumb busily working her clit, my hips burying and retreating my cock until sweat beaded on my forehead. I could barely hold off my own pleasure when she tightened even harder around me. She moaned long and hard as her pussy throbbed around my cock while she came.

As she came down off her orgasm, I bent my head and captured her nipple between my teeth once again, playing with one then the other. Each tug set her pussy pulsing around my cock, each swipe of my tongue over her breast, her shoulder, along the side of her neck, had her moaning in response.

The sweet musky scent of her arousal filling my senses, I touched her, tasted her, my cock staying still within her, though that was damned hard to accomplish. She arched and shuddered beneath me, her fingers digging into my back, my hips.

How had any man let such a responsive woman get away from him? Worse, treat her as badly as her dead husband had?

I continued my worship of her body until she begged me to "move, damn it."

Before I could react, her fingers dug deep into my butt and her hips arched beneath me, pulling me deeper inside her. Her pussy clamped around me, pulsing once more. For the life of me, I couldn't hold off anymore and I let myself go, my own orgasm driving the air from my lungs as I reveled in her heat, her welcome. Her joy.

A WEIRD CHIME FILLED THE ROOM, WAKING ME from where I lay on my bed, Ellie sprawled across me. Her hair feathered across my skin, tickling me. Her breasts pressed against my chest, making my morning woody rock hard in a heartbeat.

We'd gone three rounds last night before we'd both collapsed, sweaty and fully spent. After the last time, where Ellie had ridden me like she was a prize-winning rodeo cowgirl and I was the bucking bronco who couldn't be tamed, she'd blown out a deep breath, muttered, "You're good, Walsh. I think I'll keep you around," then slumped beside me, put her head on my shoulder and fallen asleep. As if she'd been sleeping there all her life.

The weird chime sounded again, and Ell muttered, pushed herself up and stared blearily around as if she couldn't figure out where she was. Then she blinked and gave me the most beautiful smile. "Hey, you."

I pushed her hair out of her face and lifted myself up to kiss her nose. "Hey, yourself."

That weird chime sounded again. I frowned and glanced around the room.

"It's one of my phone alarms," she announced before settling back in my arms. "Fuck it, it's Sunday. I can ignore it. If it's one of my clients, they know they won't get a response until tomorrow."

Worked for me. I gestured to my morning woody. "Do you want to go for another round of getting hot and sweaty before we shower together?"

The chime sounded again cutting off her response. She pulled away with a curse. "Shit. It's Sunday!"

A day neither of us had to work. "Yeah, so?"

"I have brunch with Mom and Josh. That's what the chime is—my calendar reminder."

Right, I'd forgotten about the Mason family tradition

of Sunday brunches, complete with French toast, waffles, and pancakes, along with a shit-ton of bacon and sausages. My mouth watered at the memory. Then I remembered the significance of today's brunch. "When you're telling Josh about us."

About how I had already broken my promise to keep her at arm's length. As I held her, loving how she'd felt in my arms, in my bed, I had to admit that if it came to a choice between Josh and Ellie, I knew who I'd choose.

She scrambled off the bed and searched for her clothes. "Yeah, and he's picking me up in about a half hour..."

"So you need to leave before he discovers you not there and sets out to find you."

Clutching her discarded clothes to her chest, she nodded slowly. "I'm sorry."

"No need to be."

As she dressed, I swung out of bed and gathered my clothes where I'd discarded them. "Maybe I should go with you."

She paused, straightening with her hands still behind her back as she fastened her bra. Then she shook her head. "No. I think it's better if it's just us. You being there might be like taunting him and cause more drama."

True, but if Josh was going to be an ass—which I'd seen him be in the past—she shouldn't be the one to face his ire. Josh had his narcissistic moments, his need for control, that I'd learned to ignore, but the idea that he might try to control Ellie, over any of her decisions, set my teeth on edge. Had Ellie accepted Gareth's control because Josh had trained her it was normal?

Ellie finished fastening her bra and was tugging her shirt

over her head as she said, "I can handle Josh. Don't worry. Plus, Mom will be there to keep him in line."

I nodded slowly. "All right, but call me and tell me how it went when you get home."

She promised.

I stopped before I opened her SUV's door, kissing her long and hard again. "Remember, it's your life, your decision who you date, or who you don't."

She rolled her eyes. "I know. I've got this, okay?"

At my grudging nod, she lifted herself on tiptoes and kissed the tip of my nose, then reached around and patted my butt. "How about I come back here after brunch and I can take you up on that shower suggestion?"

I'm no dummy. I agreed. With interest.

CHAPTER ELEVEN

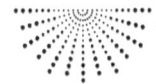

On Tuesday, I was cleaning the numerous windows in the garden room. Mindless chores like cleaning, or dusting, or even loading the dishwasher often helped me work through thorny issues. And boy, did I have an issue.

I hadn't lied when I told Malcolm I planned to tell Josh about us dating during the family Sunday brunch, but I'd never managed to get a word in edgewise. Josh had been buzzed about some new client he'd acquired who would bring a lot of business. He and Mom had spent the whole brunch discussing how to keep the new client as well as how to find more. I'd ended up leaving early, and from the text I'd received that evening they hadn't noticed I'd left until hours later. I'd tried phoning Josh the next day, but he'd been brusque, promised to call me when he had a chance, and hung up.

"Tax season. You know how it is," he'd explained.

I did, but he hadn't phoned so I used the bonus time to figure out exactly how I'd tell him about Mal, and how to ensure Josh realized it was none of his business.

When the doorbell rang, I wiped my hands on one of the rags, tossed it onto the counter and hurried to the front door.

Staring out over the road, with a peace lily tucked under one arm, was a woman with gray liberally sprinkled through her dark hair, and Malcolm's dark eyes, though she had a lot more laugh lines at the edges.

"Hey, Louise! Come on in!" I opened the door wider and stepped back to allow Malcolm's mother entry.

Where my mom favored business clothes—dark suits, white blouses and low-heeled pumps, Louise always wore loose shirts with flowy sleeves straight out of the seventies. Today, in addition to a flowery tunic, she wore black yoga pants and a pair of brown leather Birkenstocks. With hand-knitted socks. And, as usual for her, a chunky necklace made up of green and gray stones that probably had some sort of meaning behind them and matched the dangly earrings that completed her outfit.

She held out the plant. "I bought you a housewarming present."

I blinked. "But you..." I glanced through the living room to the peace lily Malcolm had brought over. The one he'd said was from his mother.

She must have followed my gaze. "Oh, you've got one already. Well, now you have two. You can never have too many peace lilies in a house, especially a place this size. They're supposed to be great air cleaners."

"Yes, I've heard that about them." *From your son.* As I took the plant and placed it on the mantel beside the other one, she followed me.

Once I faced her again, she tilted her head. "How have you been, sweetie?"

She had that tone everyone greeted with me these days. The "I'm so sorry you're a widow" tone.

"I'm fine," I stressed. "Seriously, don't worry about me."

I don't know why I didn't stop there. Maybe because I trusted Louise more than I did most people, and now I'd started, the truth surged out of me like the water over Niagara Falls. Besides, it wasn't fair to expect Malcolm to keep my secrets. "Things weren't great between Gareth and I toward the end anyway. I was planning on asking him for a divorce. To be honest, him dying was easier for me than if I'd had to divorce him."

She blinked and her mouth formed an O, but she didn't say anything, simply took my hand and squeezed it lightly. "Does your mother know?"

"She knows."

Did Louise know I was dating her son? Or similar to how he was waiting for me to inform my family we were dating, should I wait for him to inform his? Maybe I should text him to ask. I straightened my shoulders. "Would you like some tea or coffee? I picked up some butter tarts from Portside Pastries."

Louise beamed. "Portside? I am not about to turn them down."

She followed me into the kitchen and while I waited for

the kettle to boil (plugged into a different outlet than the microwave this time) and she plated a butter tart on each of the plates I'd handed her, I filled her in on my plans for the house.

"When I was a little, I used to imagine buying it when I was grown and how I'd turn it into a B&B." It wasn't until after Gareth and I were engaged that I learned it was owned by Gareth's grandmother. She hadn't been able to make it to his funeral, so she'd invited me to visit her when I felt up to it. Which had been a month after my first visit with my therapist. Ruby had been so happy to see me, probably to have any visitors since she'd been housebound her final days. We'd spent hours chatting about what it was like to grow up in Port Paxton during the war, about her husband and his family who had built Hauser House. And, occasionally, about Gareth's father, who apparently had been nothing like his son. One visit turned into two, then a third, and soon dropping in for tea became a regular occasion every time I visited my parents, which had become a weekly trip. When Grandma Ruby died eight months after Gareth, I'd been shocked to learn she'd left her entire estate to me.

Louise frowned. "My friend Bea, the lady who made that quilt I gave you for your thirtieth birthday? A couple years back, she and her wife tried to get the zoning on their place changed. They went through hell trying to jump through all the town council's hoops. Never did end up getting permission."

"That's what I discovered. Plus, there's the whole having-to-let-strangers-into-my-home thing and I realized I can't do it. I've been here less than a week and I feel safer here because I'm alone." I frowned at how that made me sound paranoid. "It's hard to explain."

"Maybe because your husband isn't likely to walk in the door?"

I shrugged. "That's what my therapist suggested, too." We'd talked a lot during our last video session, about Malcolm and my fears about letting someone else in my life. I decided not to think about that while Louise was watching me. I made my voice light and said, "I could always set up some yurts on the back field and rent them out in the summer."

Louise laughed. "Oh honey, the way the storms come across the lake? They'll pick up those tents and send them flying clear over to Rochester."

"There is that."

As we sipped tea and nibbled on the butter tarts, we chatted about the changes to the town since I'd last lived here. Changes like the big box store being built on the outskirts to satisfy all the cottagers who surrounded the lake when they came back in the spring to discover they needed to do repairs after their cottages had been empty. How the bakery had changed hands and the new owners had added a couple of tables and served coffee and sandwiches too, mainly to the tourists. Louise gushed over the used bookshop, and the new wool shop that also gave lessons on how to spin yarn. Which was her latest obsession.

In the middle of her description about a visit she'd made to an alpaca farm the previous year, she stopped mid-sentence, placed her hand on mine and said, "Here I am yammering on. I never asked if I was interrupting you. You work from home, right?"

"I would have let you know. And I'm really happy you stopped by."

She glanced away, as if she were afraid to meet my eyes. "I have to admit, I'm not here for completely selfless reasons. A friend of mine saw you having dinner with Malcolm in Peterborough the other night. Are you two dating?"

Crap. "I don't think one dinner counts as dating as such, but we're exploring the possibilities," I admitted slowly.

She frowned. "You say that as if you're skittish because you're still dealing with the aftermath of Gareth's abuse."

Figured that I couldn't get anything past her. "Yes. And no. I've got a really good therapist," I hurried to assure her. "And she says I'm ready to date, I mean it's been nearly two years since Gareth died, but dating Malcolm? It's...strange, you know?"

"Like you got used to walking on eggshells around Gareth, and you think you have to around Malcolm?"

I started to shake my head, that I knew Malcolm wasn't Gareth, but maybe she had a point. "Maybe? But mainly because it's Malcolm. And I don't want to screw this up. I don't want to lose him as a friend if things go south."

"Have you told him? About what Gareth did?"

I nodded. "He knows. He was great. He's so supportive, you know?"

"That's what the right person is supposed to do in a relationship." She clasped my hand. "If you think Malcolm's the right one, if you trust him, then go for it. But if he doesn't treat you right, tell someone. Your mom. Me. Someone. And definitely your therapist. Don't try to be strong and think you have to deal with it all yourself. I know I'm his mother but I'm here for you, too."

"Thanks, Louise." Damned if the waterworks didn't start up.

CHAPTER TWELVE

MALCOLM

I stared Ellie's text and tried to decipher if there was some hidden message within it.

ELLIE

Your mom visited. She knows we went on a date. One of her friends saw us in Peterborough.

Nope, not that I could tell. Mom asked her if we were dating. Which we were. Especially since we'd spent every night together since that date. Mom would probably be over the moon that I was dating again. I had been dating before Ellie though I wasn't in the habit of sharing who I was dating with my mom. But me dating Ellie? Color her one pleased mother.

The only concern I'd had was Josh, and nothing had happened after Ellie had told her family on Sunday, so even he wasn't an issue anymore. So yeah, no biggie.

I texted back "Great" and then upon reflection added, "Want me to bring home a pizza tonight?"

My phone dinged seconds later.

ELLIE

No pizza. I was thinking burgers on the grill. I cleaned it and got the propane tank filled. Yes, you can be the Burgermeister

Ha! A woman after my own heart. How did she know I loved firing up the grill? No doubt my mother had given her a heads up, probably telling her the tale of me barbecuing hamburgers during a blizzard in January a couple years back. Sometimes Mom's interference wasn't such a bad thing.

The last job of the day left me sweaty and dirty. After I'd parked in Ellie's driveway, I stared at my reflection in my newly repaired truck's rearview mirror, deciding if I should have gone home to shower first. Then I remembered how Ellie and I had showered together yesterday morning, and the day before that, and how we'd both ended up needing to shower again after some mad lovemaking. Having Ellie soap me up and get all the dirt off of me before handing me the tongs for the grill would definitely be a great date.

"You just going to stand there or are you coming in?" Ellie stood on the porch, leaning against one of the fluted columns. Her hair was loose today, swirling about her shoulders. Her bright-yellow shirt made her shine like the sun, the fabric taut across her breasts, the same way her black yoga pants hugged her hips. Both of which I'd spent a lot of time paying special attention to last night. And if I had my way, would again in a few minutes.

With a huff of impatience, she walked down the step and across the lawn toward me, her expression as predatory as I suspected mine was. Her gaze swept down me, lingering on my crotch, which reacted with interest. She reached out to touch me but I stepped back, and hurt replaced the need in her eyes.

I held up my hand to display the dirt embedded in my skin. "I've been crawling around in fibreglass all day." And touching oily pipes and years of mice droppings but I didn't think she'd want to hear that extra detail. "You do not want me to touch you right now. Want to help me shower though?"

The interest that had faded flared back into her eyes and she gave me a coquettish look. "Because you're such a dirty boy?"

My momma didn't raise no fool. I leered at her and nodded. "Yup. Want to clean me up, dirty girl?"

As she followed me to the main bathroom, she said, "I had a nice talk with your mom today."

Which she'd already told me in the earlier texts. Or was there something she hadn't included? I decided to keep it light. "Let me guess, she wants to rent your back field so she can keep alpacas?"

She laughed. "D'you know I wondered if she might ask that. She's so passionate about her spinning."

"She's always needed to keep busy." I stripped off my t-shirt and tossed it in the empty hamper. The grocery basket I kept my dirty clothes in at my place was overflowing. I really needed to do laundry one of these days, especially if I wanted to invite her over to my place again. Maybe if stopping off at her place became a regular event, I needed to keep a set of clean clothes here?

As I turned on the water, Ellie leaned against the door frame, watching me, mirroring what she'd done on the porch. "Your mom bought me a peace lily. Said it was a housewarming present."

She tilted her head and raised an eyebrow in a "gotcha" look that mirrored one her mother had given me when she caught me and Josh snitching some fresh-baked brownies she'd made for the school bake sale.

Then Ellie's gaze lowered and laser-beamed on my crotch which made my cock twitch and harden at her attention. "Go on then. Don't get all shy now. It's not like I haven't soaped up your Johnson before."

I checked the water temperature, then stepped into the shower, but out of range of the spray. "Wasn't that the plan this time?" I cocked an eyebrow at her. "And why are you still dressed?"

With a laugh, she lifted her shirt over her head, ditched her yoga pants, and stepped into the shower with me. Her breasts brushed my elbow as she bent to pump some liquid soap into her hand. I had to remind myself that my hands were still laden with oil and fiberglass so I shouldn't play with those beautiful D-cup breasts until I'd fully cleaned up. So I grabbed the bar of soap on the soap rack and cleaned them off. It wasn't as good as the orange stuff I used to get the worst of the grunge off but it wasn't bad. I'd brought it over yesterday when I'd discovered her special soaps—like the one she was coating my chest with—did dick-all in cutting through grease.

I swore when her soapsuds-covered hands captured my dick and stroked my rigid shaft. My knees weakened, forcing me to lean against the tile as she tightened her hold and stroked faster, her thumb flicking over the sensitive head. The last time she'd jerked me off in the shower, she'd ended up on her knees, me coming in her mouth. This time, she leaned in, her breasts brushing my chest and whispered, "Let me watch you come." Then she lifted my hand and placed it over hers. Her eyes widened, her pupils darkening, when I increased the pressure and stroked harder.

I placed my free hand on her breast and rolled the nipple between my thumb and forefinger. Her breath stuttered and the rhythm of her hand around my cock would have been lost if I hadn't been guiding its path. From the way her hips bucked, I figured she was close to coming herself, even without me touching her. That was enough to tip me over the edge. I barked out another curse and came hard, shooting a thick stream between us, coating us both.

Both of us breathing hard, I loosened my hand from over hers, and she released my still hard cock. She glanced down at it and raised an eye brow. "I'm impressed. It looks like you could go another round even now."

After a quick duck under the shower to rinse off the remaining soap and ensuring my hands were indeed clean, I turned her around so her back pressed against the tile, lifted one of her legs at the knee and wrapped it around my waist. I caught her mouth with mine at the same time I thrust deep inside her.

Our moans mingled as my hips thrust a rapid pace, her sweet pussy clenching me, wet and welcoming. I reached between us and found her clit, thumbing it in a mixture of strokes until she came hard. Her calling my name was the sexiest thing I'd ever heard, making me harder and ready to come again.

The bathroom door flung open, hitting the wall beside the shower. Josh stood there, his eyes widening, fist clenching and his brows lowering in anger. "Get off her, Walsh, you fucking bastard."

Ellie squeaked and grabbed at the towel she'd hung over the shower stall, wrapping it around her and yelling, "Get out!"

Since Ellie had grabbed the only towel at hand, I stood there, buck-ass naked, my Johnson glistening with Ellie's juices, still standing proud like the fucking CN Tower, though it was quickly retreating and would soon hang limp like a flag on a windless day.

"You motherfucking traitor!" Josh grabbed the shower door open and lunged for me. I don't know if he deliberately pushed Ellie to the side or if she tried to intercept him, but she ended up smashing against the back wall of the stall, hitting her head on the tile, her feet going out from under her.

Keeping an eye on Josh to ensure he didn't continue his assault, I knelt beside her, checking to ensure she hadn't hurt anything.

Josh backed off, swearing how sorry he was, that he hadn't meant to hurt Ellie. Right up until she got back on her feet, and then he started up with the questions about how the fuck could she betray him like this.

What the actual fuck. How had *she* betrayed *him?* I could see him coming after me, but going after his own sister and accusing *her* of betrayal? What had gone on during the Sunday brunch that she hadn't told me about?

"Get out of my bathroom, Josh," Ellie snapped. "In fact, get out of my house and don't come back unless you're invited."

———

AFTER I'D SLAMMED THE BATHROOM DOOR SHUT and locked it this time, I checked her head for any cuts, but couldn't anything, not even a hint of a goose egg. I held up one finger and, mimicking the television docs, told her to follow my finger and drew it back and forth. I didn't really know what I was supposed to be seeing but I figured that as long as she tracked the movement, it might be a good sign. Still, I asked, "Do you need to see a doctor?"

"No, I'm fine." She caught my hand and clutched it to her chest. "I'm sorry, Mal. I didn't get a chance to tell them we were dating on Sunday. They were so caught up talking about the changes in this year's tax codes I couldn't get a word in edgewise."

Despite her protest that she was fine, I picked her up and carried her to her bed, ignoring Josh who was stalking the upstairs hallway, then returned to the bathroom where I grabbed my work pants, hopping as I pulled them on. I'd have to shower again but that was small potatoes compared to this situation.

As I headed back to Ellie's bedroom, Josh faced me, his fists clenched, his entire face as red as his hair.

"Ellie told you to leave," I growled.

"Not until I've had this out with Ellie. And you."

Aware of Ellie getting dressed in the bedroom, and trying to spare her the venom in her brother's voice, I narrowed my eyes at him and gestured toward the stairs with my chin. "Not here. Downstairs. On the porch."

"What?" he sneered. "You think you need witnesses when I beat your ass?"

As if. Josh may have adrenaline and righteous anger going for him, but we both knew who would win in a fistfight and it wasn't him. "Ellie needs to know this house is her safe zone and right now, you're not keeping her safe. So if we're going to get into this, we're doing it outside."

His gaze flickered past me and his lips thinned. Then he turned and stalked downstairs, me hot on his heels. The moment he hit the porch, he wheeled around and turned on me.

"You fucking promised me you'd leave her alone. You gave me your word—guess you proved that's worth shit, isn't it?"

"For fuck's sake, we were sixteen. We're not kids anymore. Ellie is perfectly capable of making her own decisions."

"And look where that got her. She ended up with that fucking son-of-a-bitch who fucking cheated on her and then tried to blame her, saying she was useless in bed."

Ah. I hadn't heard that part before. I wasn't about to say her ex was completely wrong, either. No use adding fuel to Josh's self-righteous fire.

"Yeah, Mom told me. Did you know?" Josh's whole body shook, his voice cracked in rage.

I nodded. "Ellie told me."

"Eight years, she endured that fucker's treatment.

Eight. Fucking. Years. And now here I find you with her? After you promised you'd leave her alone? I'm not standing by and watching her get hurt again. Not by you, not by anyone."

"You think I'd hurt her?" I stopped myself from taking my own step forward this time. Forced my breathing and my tone to stay even against the welling betrayal. "You know me, Josh. You know I'd take a bullet for Ellie before I'd let her get hurt." My control cracked so I couldn't stop myself from blurting, "And how do you know I'm going to hurt her and not the other way around?"

"I don't give a flying fuck if you get hurt," Josh snarled. "You're not my sister."

Whoa. I got where he was coming from, but to hear such a pronouncement from the guy who had been my best friend since I could walk? It fucking hurt, man.

"Give me your word you will stay away from her," he demanded.

There it was. Time to choose.

A week ago I would have considered it to be *Sophie's Choice*, but today? There was no doubt in my mind who I chose and it wouldn't be him.

Except he didn't wait for my response. "I want you to guarantee me that if she tries to hire you to do the electrical in her house, you'll refuse the business. That you'll send her somewhere else," Josh shouted, his finger stabbing the air at me. "I don't want you to even approach her. If you even fucking *think* you see Ell on the street, you'll cross to the other side and leave her the fuck alone."

"No." My control shattered. I'd prided myself in being able to closely guard my temper, in maintaining my control.

In being the peacemaker in tense situations. But Josh had taken things a step too far.

I suspected my own face was almost as bright red as Josh's, my fists clenched. "And not just no, but hell fucking no. Ellie is a grown woman. She's a fucking smart woman too. If you try to control who she dates you're as fucking bad as her fucking former husband."

"She's. My. Sister," he bit out through clenched teeth, his color rising until he resembled a firetruck.

"Then stop trying to control her. Ask her what she wants, and then respect her opinion. You can give her advice, but then you need to step back and trust her."

"Like I did last time? I knew Gareth was wrong for her from the first time I laid eyes on him. But I stepped back then and look what happened."

Not once had I heard Josh say anything negative about his brother-in-law, but maybe in hindsight he'd realized he had seen—and ignored—some red flags and was blaming himself?

"It wasn't your fault, Josh."

We both whirled at the sound of Ellie's voice.

CHAPTER THIRTEEN

MALCOLM

"It wasn't my fault either," Ellie said, her voice firm and steady. "Gareth played us all. He knew how to behave in public, how to look like he was such a great guy. Abusers are like that. You weren't the only one to fall for his charade. But d'you honestly think I've been crying into my pillow and playing the victim for the last two years? No." She stepped down off the porch and stood beside me, taking my hand in hers. As much as I appreciated her silent show of support, I couldn't miss the glower Josh gave me when he noticed it too.

"I've had therapy, Josh. I'm still in therapy," she continued. "I've learned the signs when someone's gaslighting me. I'm not going to be a victim again. I've got a support system in place." She took few deep breaths. "I appreciate you think you need to stick up for me, and I'll welcome your opinion. But it stops here."

"Ell—" Josh stammered.

She shook her head. "No. It's my turn to talk, and your turn to listen."

He closed his eyes and grimaced before nodding with a whispered, "All right."

"How do you think I feel about my brother busting into *my* bathroom in *my* house because he doesn't approve of me having an adult relationship? To know that you're ready to punch out your best friend because you're trying to control what we—" she circled her finger between me and herself "—do?"

"Ell—"

"No. How dare you demand he walk away? Mal is right. By controlling him, you're controlling *me*. How do you think that makes me feel about you, huh?"

"I'm trying to protect you. That's my job as your big brother."

She shook her head. "You have a problem with a choice I make, you talk to *me*. We discuss it. Calmly. Rationally. You're welcome to make your argument, but just because I listen won't mean I'll agree with you. I make a decision you don't like? Tough shit. Even if I'm wrong, I have to make my own mistakes." Her voice cracked so I tightened my grip on her hand briefly, showing her my support. She squeezed it back and resumed. "Threatening Mal? Bullying him? Telling him that you're only thinking of me? That you're trying to help me better myself? That's what Gareth used to say."

Josh glanced at me before focusing back on his sister. "Are you sure about this, Ell? That Mal's the one you want to jump back into the dating pool with?"

"Yes. I'm positive. In fact, why aren't you? Mal's been

your best friend our whole lives. You know he's a good guy. You know he would never hurt me. You knew I was interested in him back in high school, and I think you know that he was interested in me too, weren't you? That's why you forced him to make that stupid promise, isn't it?"

He glanced away, not at me, nor at Ellie, then gave a tiny nod. "Brian Cawkers saw you kissing him and told me." He swallowed hard. "You were so young, Ellie. So naive. I was looking out for you."

"I'm only eighteen months younger than you, you big dipwad," she said dryly. "We grew up in the same family, attended the same schools, experienced the same things. If I was naive, so were you."

"I'm your older brother. I'm supposed to take care of you." Josh's voice took on a whiny nasally tone, one I hadn't heard in years.

"Maybe when I was kid. But now I'm all grown-up and capable of making my own decisions." She huffed out a breath. "Go home, Josh. I know you still have a lot of questions, but not tonight, okay? Call me tomorrow and we'll arrange to have dinner or something."

He wavered, opened his mouth a few times as if he wanted to argue more, then grumbled, "All right," and climbed into his car.

Ellie's chin dropped to her chest but since she was facing away from me, I couldn't read her expression. Hopefully she didn't feel that she needed to gather courage to face me.

When she did turn around, she lifted one shoulder in a half-hearted shrug. "He means well."

"I know." I forced a grin to hide the emotions welling inside. "So I'm your boyfriend, huh?"

"You caught that, did you?" She wrapped her arms around me. "You said you wouldn't see anyone else while we're together, so yeah. You're my boyfriend."

"It's a big step." Was she ready? I didn't want to rush her into a relationship that she might regret later.

She caught her bottom lip between her teeth as she considered it. "Not really. Josh might have made you promise to walk away back in high school but I don't think I ever stopped being interested in you."

"But you married Gareth."

"You were with Natalie."

Shit.

"Don't look like that." She rolled her eyes. "I told you I dated other guys before Gareth, remember?"

She laced her fingers with mine and tugged me toward her front door. "Come on, I promised you burgers. Let's get your apron on, Burgermeister, and fire up the grill."

ELLIE

I snuggled against Malcolm, his arm draped over my shoulder on the patio, the plates with our burgers and the salad I'd prepared on the table in front of us, the scent of the barbequed meat still filling the air. After Josh had left, conversation with Mal had been strained, me asking about what project he'd worked on today, him asking if I'd gotten any more quotes from the roofers I'd contacted. Eventually he'd loosened up and asked me how my job was going and the project I'd been working on, especially about one particularly obstreperous client I'd complained to him about two nights before. Gareth had never asked about my work. Which reminded me...

"By the way, thank you."

Mal shook his head, his expression one of puzzlement. "For what?"

"For not stepping in between me and Josh and duking it out," I explained. "For letting me handle him."

"I wanted to," he grumbled. "Especially after you fell because of him. People have died falling in their tubs."

"I know," I acknowledged. "Which is why I'm thanking you."

He grunted and took another bite of his burger.

"You don't get it, do you?"

He shook his head, but didn't speak since he was still chewing.

"You let me stand up for myself." I didn't have to say *the way Gareth never would have let me* because I didn't have to. Malcolm got it. After I'd asked him to back off, he had. He may have been silent, watching and ready to jump in to help if I'd needed it, but he trusted me enough to handle it myself.

"It about fucking killed me." He dropped the hamburger back on the plate but wouldn't look at me, staring at the burger instead. "I'm so scared of scaring you off. Of making you think I'm like that motherfucking husband of yours."

Oh shit. "You are nothing like him. Tonight proved it."

I caught his free hand between mine. "We're in the early

days yet. We may have known each other our whole lives but we're still learning about each other. If you do something that pisses me off, I need to be able to tell you what's wrong, and you need to listen to me."

He shook his head. "That's the way I've always tried to work. With you. With my clients. My family. I thought you knew that."

I did. "But it works the other way around too. I'm going to do things that piss you off too. And you need to talk to me—not retreat and close yourself off. No silent treatment. We talk things out."

He raised his eyebrows at me. "I don't do the silent treatment so no worries there."

"We both need to remember that every day we're together, we're going to change. And not necessarily in the same way, for the same reasons. If this relationship is to survive, we need to work as a team. Neither one of us is better than the other. Sometimes you're going to be right, and sometimes I will be. Sometimes we'll both be right, just in different ways. As long as we can both agree to that, I think we can be okay."

"Wisdom according to your therapist?"

"Wisdom according to your mother."

He huffed a laugh. "I guess since Mom and Dad celebrated their forty-first last month, they must know what they're talking about."

"I think it's good advice." Had Louise given my parents the same advice and been ignored? Is that part of why my parents had divorced?

He lifted his hand, the one I was holding, and kissed my knuckles. "I can't read minds, so I hope if I miss any clues, you'll come right out and tell me." He pursed his lips. "Actually, come right out and say things rather than leaving clues. Even if you think it'll upset me. If we are honest with each other, if we can be each other's sounding boards, I think we'll be good together."

I leaned my forehead against his and whispered, "I think we *are* good together."

He kissed the top of my head. "So do I."

EPILOGUE

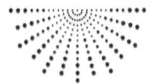

ELLIE

I pulled into the driveway of Hauser House a little too fast and parked my SUV beside Malcolm's half ton. Once I turned off the ignition, I leaned back in my seat and scowled at the envelope I'd tossed on the seat. I hated the damned contract Sheila had handed me. Hated what it represented, even if, according to my financial advisor, it was in my best interest. It wasn't best for Malcolm, and he was the best thing I had in my life. Had *ever* had in my life. He'd proven that numerous times over the past year. In his willingness to listen to my ideas, to offer suggestions without demanding I follow them. In how he'd made French toast for me every Saturday morning and served it to me in bed most times. Turned out he was a better cook than I'd ever been.

I loved how he knew when to make me laugh and when not to, in bed or out. I loved how he didn't pressure me to marry him, knowing that would be the fastest way for me to freeze up. I even loved that he'd met Rebecca and attended a few therapy sessions with me.

I especially loved it when he made love to me. Loved the way he looked at me with complete adoration as he undressed me, or while I undressed him. Loved the way his palms skimmed over my belly, or cupped my breasts, worshiping them, worshiping me. The feel of his beard between my thighs when he went down on me was almost enough to make me come without the aid of his tongue and fingers. None of that compared to how much I loved when he was buried deep within me.

Which was why that damned contract Sheila had pressed on me felt like a betrayal. Of Malcolm. And of us.

I'd moved in with Malcolm the day before the first contractor had arrived to tear out the kitchen last September. Malcolm's prediction about supply and equipment delays and contractors' constantly changing schedules had been correct, interfering with my grand plans of renovating this magnificent Victorian home. Yesterday, almost a year to the day I'd faced an electrical meltdown and Malcolm came back into my life, we'd both moved back in to Hauser House—which I was considering renaming. Not that the locals would refer to it by its new name. To them, it would always be Hauser House, the same way the Rogers Centre will always be the SkyDome to most Torontonians.

Across the lake, heavy dark storm clouds with a curtain of rain shrouded the sun, and thunder rumbled in the distance. As much as I love watching thunderstorms, I don't like being outside in them so I grabbed the legal envelope I'd tossed on the passenger seat, folded it and stuffed it in my purse, and raced to the cover of the verandah.

Once inside, I used my heel to kick the freshly painted front door closed. As I hung up my jacket in the closet and dumped my purse on the side table, I called, "Malcolm? I'm home!"

No cheery "hey!" that had become Malcolm's usual greeting echoed down the hallway.

Huh, that was strange. His truck was in the driveway, so he was here. Somewhere.

I called out again.

Still no answer.

With the storm coming in across the light, even though the sun wouldn't set for another hour, the clouds turned the house gloomy so I switched on the hallway chandelier. Light blazed, hundreds of prisms sparkling across the hall, into the living room, and up the stairs. The ornate Victorian chandelier had turned out to be original to the house, with 24 bulbs and too many Baccarat crystals to count. After Malcolm had taken the fixture down to update the wiring and I'd realized it was in desperate need of a cleaning so made it my mission to clean each individual crystal and had tried counting them but lost track. I also discovered it was worth several thousand dollars, according to an appraiser. Josh had encouraged me to accept their offer and buy something more energy efficient. As if.

Its light made the newly sanded and stained floor shine too, and highlighted the new paint on all the walls and ceilings.

I wandered to our brand-new country kitchen with its

gleaming quartz countertop, double built-in ovens, and the island I'd dreamed off since I was a teen. But no Malcolm.

I peered out the window to the back yard, to see if he was doing yard work or maybe grilling dinner. Which would be dangerous with the oncoming storm. Maybe he was putting away the lawn furniture to stop it from being picked up by the winds that were now fiercely whipping the trees. But no joy there either.

"Malcolm?" I called again. Worry started to niggle at me. What if he'd fallen or something? I opened the basement door but there were no lights on down there. Malcolm hated that basement and never went down without turning on the lights, and usually kept a flashlight on hand "just in case." I flicked on the lights—he'd added one at the top and the bottom of the stairs in addition to changing out the single swinging lightbulb that had been the lone source of light down there. I blew out a breath when I didn't see him lying unresponsive at the base of the stairs.

Maybe he was having a shower and fell? I hurried up the stairs to our bedroom and the massive new ensuite we'd had installed. Empty.

Then I heard something, a small sound, a scuff like a footstep directly overhead. Ah. He must be up in the turret room we'd fitted out to be my office. I went back out into the hallway and opened the small wooden door that revealed the narrow staircase leading upstairs. Malcolm was there, standing in front of one of the windows, overlooking the bay.

I leaned against the doorframe, watching him, admiring

him. His hair was longer now, almost touching his shoulders. His beard was longer too—at my urging.

A jagged flash of fork lightning backlit him as it struck something on the island in the middle of Hawkeshead Lake. On its heels, a loud roll of thunder boomed across the water, shaking the window panes.

I must have made a sound because Malcolm turned and noticed me, a smile melting his face. "Hey, Ell. Done for the day?"

"Yup." I took another step into the room, finally noticing the dozens of candles he'd set out on the mantel of the fireplace we'd had restored to keep the room warm in the winter, along with the massive barrel chair I'd pointed out to him six months before. He'd placed it in the curve of the windows, facing out over the lake, exactly where I would have chosen.

He followed my gaze and his grin broadened. "Surprise."

I walked to the chair, running a hand across the back, over the pillows. It was exactly the color and fabric choice I'd wanted. "How did you get this up the stairs?"

He shrugged in his usual aw-shucks manner. "You said you always wanted to be able to curl up here with a good book or to watch the thunderstorms roll across the lake. More than once. So I figured it would be a nice Welcome Home gift for you."

I started to tell him that hadn't answered my question but another lightning bolt struck, causing the lights to flicker. I held my breath, counting—this time I didn't even get to two before the thunder rattled the windows.

Malcolm stepped behind me and wrapped his arms

around my waist, pulling him against him as we watched the sheet of rain crawl across the lake, obscuring the island, and head straight for us.

"Good thing you got some candles lit already," I muttered.

"Power won't go out, remember? We've got the generator installed. Besides the sun won't set for another hour so it won't get that dark even if the lights do go out."

"Spoilsport," I muttered.

"What?" He tilted his head so he could see me better. "The generator was your idea. And it was a good one, especially in the winter."

I turned in his arms until I faced him, then hooked my arms around his neck. "I like the idea of being stuck up here with you, alone in the candlelight."

The heat in his eyes, the love filling his expression, overwhelmed me. After a year of being with him, I should be used to it by now. But every time he looked at me that way—and he looked at me like that from the moment he woke up until we fell asleep in each other's arms, plus a billion times in between—I found myself in awe.

Oh sure, we've had our arguments in the past year—like how he didn't agree with my choice in bathroom tiles or I had a different vision for the front hallway, but nothing major. I said my side. He said his. No yelling, no silent treatment, just talking until we came to an agreement. Sometimes he was right, sometimes I was, and sometimes it turned out neither of us were.

This, *this* was what love was supposed to be like.

I pressed against his groin and felt his immediate and gratifying hardness in response.

His lips twitched. "Ell? Are you trying to seduce me?"

I pointedly glanced around the room. "I'm not the one who lit all these candles." Or placed the handful of condoms on the blanket I spied beside the barrel chair. "I'd say you have some plans of your own, Mr. Walsh."

I jumped when a sizzling bolt of lightning struck something on this side of the lake with no time between the flash and the boom of thunder that made my floors shake along with the windows. "Maybe we should go down stairs."

"We're safe here." Though he tightened his grip on me and pressed a kiss to my forehead. "Don't worry."

"This is the highest spot on this side of the lake. Doesn't that make us a target? What if it hits the turret?"

"That's what the lightning rods are for, Ell. We'll be fine," he assured me. He led me to the newest addition to the room and pulled me down on his lap. We cuddled together, watching the rain lash the window panes, listening to the thunder rumbling as the storm raged outside.

"I know all the work you did to set this up, but maybe having my office up here isn't a smart idea." I hated how small my voice was.

He pressed his lips to my hair again. "Babe, when we were drawing up the plans you were all about how you wanted to sit up here and watch the storms come in."

"I know, but..." How the hell was I going to broach that damned contract? Maybe I should put it through the shredder. *Ooops, sorry, Sheila. I got mixed up.*

"I put in state-of-the-art surge suppressors for the outlets in this room. It wouldn't hurt to unplug your laptop during storms, but if it really concerns you, maybe you could turn this into a private refuge instead and we can set up an office for you in one of the other bedrooms." He gestured toward the dozens of boxes of books waiting to be installed on the bookshelves we'd installed. "Turn it into a library or something."

"But that would mean redoing the wiring in the bedroom, and you've already done so much work." Plus, he had other clients—paying clients— who came first. I'd insisted I'd pay him for the work he'd done, but he'd refused to accept my offer, especially after we'd agreed he'd move in here with me once it was all done.

"I put surge suppressors on at least one outlet in each room, in case we ever have guests. I don't want to end up facing a lawsuit if one of their devices gets fried."

I hadn't realized he'd done that. I reached up and kissed his cheek. "And you accuse me of overthinking."

"Only the best for you."

I twisted in place, hooking my arms around his shoulders and straddling his lap. That expression of heat and safety, of acceptance, hadn't faded. If anything, it heated as I squirmed to get comfortable. "You're always looking out for me, aren't you?"

"That's what you do for the people you love." He slanted his lips over mine and murmured, "I love you."

MALCOLM

I froze when Ellie's eyes filled with tears. It's not like it was the first time I'd told her I love her so what was going on with her today? First the worry about using this room as her office, and now her reaction to my statement of love?

I settled my hands on her hips and pulled her closer. "What's going on?"

"I love you, too. You know that, right?"

"Of course." She'd said it enough times to me too. In the shower this morning. Then again at breakfast. And more hurriedly before she dashed out the door to a meeting a half hour later. And the look in her eyes when she said it was like she knew I was worthy of her love. Something I'd never really felt with any of my previous girlfriends, not even Natalie. "So what's wrong?"

"You know my meeting this morning?"

"The one with your financial advisor? Yeah."

She blushed, as she had each time anyone mentioned her finances. It was like she was ashamed of having enough money to be independent. And then some. When Josh had told me she'd never have to work again if she didn't want to, he hadn't been kidding. He'd underestimated the seven figures she was now worth.

"What did Sheila say?" Shit. I stiffened. "Tell me she didn't make some bad investment and lost all your money."

She huffed a laugh. "No, nothing like that. After we finished going through her report, she asked me how the renovations were going. I mentioned how they were all finished and we'd finally moved back in, right?"

I nodded, not wanting to interrupt her.

Her lips pursed together until they were nearly white. "She suggested I ask you to sign a cohabitation agreement. One where you agree that you have no claim on Hauser House or any of my savings and I owe you nothing should we split up."

I nodded. "Okay. That's reasonable."

I wasn't surprised that the subject had come up, only that it had come from Sheila and not Josh or Ellie's mother. Unless they'd had a private talk with Sheila and asked her to suggest it so Ell wouldn't turn on them?

I cupped my fingers beneath Ell's chin and lifted it until she met my gaze. God, I loved this woman. I loved how she cared about others, cared about me. About us. "I promise I have no plans on going after Hauser House or any of your inheritance, but Sheila is right. It's safer for you to get that in writing. I've got no problems signing an agreement."

She made a very un-Ell-like growl that, for some obscure reason, turned me on. Or maybe it was a hint of the perfume she'd dabbed on after our shower. Or maybe it was her shampoo. Any of her scents got me hard. "I told her you would say that. And frankly, I should be signing one for you to protect your company, but that's not my point."

"What is your point?" I asked, keeping my voice gentle and telling my dick to back off.

"You know I trust you, right? That I know you're not with me because my bank account is bigger than yours? You know that I don't need a damned cohabitation agreement?"

"I know," I squeezed her hands, "but I'm happy to sign one."

She slapped her hand against my chest. "It's not about

the damned agreement, Mal. She thinks you're only with me because of my money. It's like she thinks you're a...a..."

"Boy toy?" I suggested. "Trophy wife?" That earned me a laugh, which is what I'd intended. "Ell. I love you. I have no designs on this house or your money. What happens to either is totally up to you."

"I hate that people think of you as a leech," she grumbled, though she allowed me to pull her against my chest and nestled her head on my shoulder.

"It doesn't bother me. The only opinion I'm concerned about is yours."

"I know you said you're okay with us not getting married yet," she said slowly. She straddled my lap, the movement rubbing her mound against my cock. I could feel her lips curl as she felt it too. "But after all this talk about *cohabiting*? I realized I *want* to get married."

I swallowed hard. A few weeks ago, she'd made a comment about an engagement ring in the local jewelry store window and how pretty it was. During a lunch break the next day, even though I knew she wasn't ready to discuss marriage, I'd put a down payment on it and had them put it aside for me. I figured even if we never went through with a ceremony, I could give it to her as a Christmas present. Or have them change the setting into a pendant or something. Now here she was, asking me to marry her. Which, given her previous marriage, was a huge leap of faith. In me. In us.

I choked out, "Are you proposing to me?"

She nodded. "Yes. I am." When I didn't immediately answer, she added. "I know it's supposed to be you proposing to me, but I've been saying the entire year I didn't want to get married and I figured you wouldn't. Not yet."

"You know I don't need a piece of paper to wave in people's faces to prove I love you, or that I'm committed to you."

"I know. But I *want* us to get married, Mal," she said, her voice firmer than it had been the first time. "I don't want to just live with you. I don't want to introduce you as my significant other or my partner any more. I want you to be my husband. I want you to know that I trust you. That I love you." She leaned her forehead against mine. "Because I do."

"You're sure about this?"

Another nod. "We don't have to get married right away. We can wait a year or even two if you want. And we don't have to have a big ceremony. If you want to get married at the town hall, that's okay with me."

I didn't want to wait, but I didn't want a huge wedding like she'd had the first time. Even she had admitted she hadn't known most of the people who had been invited, they'd been her mother's or Gareth's friends—read business acquaintances.

I glanced across her back yard just as the first drops of rain pelted the windows. An idea slowly formed. "We could build a gazebo in the back yard, overlooking the lake. Get married in it." God, why was it so hard to speak, and why were my eyes prickling? This woman was so fricking brave. So forgiving, so loving. "We could invite our family and friends, keep it small as we take our vows out there next summer." Give her a chance to change her mind if she wanted."

"Just invite people who matter to us," she whispered.

"Yes."

She cupped my face in her palms, her eyes sparkling with unshed tears. "Yes to inviting only the people who matter, or yes you'll marry me?"

"Yes, I'll marry you. I'll even sign whatever prenup you want."

"One that we never have to invoke." With that declaration, she kissed me, her scent enveloping me, the softness of her breasts pressing against my chest making my dick hard as a rock, which only got harder as she moved rhythmically on top of me. I slid my hand beneath her skirt, pushed her panties to the side and found her wet and ready.

Her movement stuttered, so I shifted our positions and laid her on her back, her legs sprawled open to either side of my body. Our gazes met, her lips glistening, her lipstick smeared in a way that might make her squeak in embarrassment and worry about wiping it off her face if she saw her reflection, but I loved the visual proof that we'd kissed. Not breaking her gaze, I tugged her panties off, Ell lifting her hips in silent approval. Then I buried my head beneath her skirt and tasted her pussy, as I drove her with tongue and fingers until her body quivered, her breath hitched, and I knew she was on the cusp of an orgasm.

I undid my jeans and slid them down to my knees, grabbed one of the condoms I'd left on the blanket and rolled it on my erection. The barrel chair was a weird configuration, rounded, so it took some maneuvering, but I ended up pulling her until her butt was at the edge of the cushion, and positioned myself at her entrance.

"I love you, Ell. I always have, and I always will." With

that declaration, I buried myself inside her. I loved watching our bodies join this way. Ell made a carnal noise as her core clamped around me. Keeping one hand between us, my fingers stroking her clit, I leaned over her, caught her mouth again and pumped hard, knowing how she liked it, driving her to orgasm again.

When I finally slumped on top of her, she turned her head against my neck and said,

"I love you too, Mal."

Her declaration, one I'd heard hundreds of times over the past year, with no kissing, no movement to encourage me, set off another orgasm for us both. An overpowering bliss that proved the initial spark of attraction that had flared between us a year ago now blazed with an incandescence that consumed us, joined us. An attraction that wound itself around my heart and fused me to Ellie's. Forever and always.

ABOUT LEAH BRAEMEL

Married to her college sweetheart, and the proud mother of two sons, and grandmother to three beautiful (and lively) grandsons, Leah Braemel is the only woman in a houseful of men—even their dog and cat are male. She loves escaping the ever-multiplying dust bunnies by opening up her laptop to write about sexy heroes and the women who challenge them.

Sign up for Leah's newsletter by scanning the QR code or visiting her website LeahBraemel.com

facebook.com/AuthorLeahBraemel

instagram.com/LeahBraemel

bookbub.com/authors/leah-braemel

OTHER BOOKS BY LEAH BRAEMEL

BARNETT SPRINGS ROMANCES

Texas Tangle

Tangled Past

Feeding the Flames

Texas Hook-Up

HAUBERK PROTECTION SERIES

First Night

Private Property

Personal Protection

Deliberate Deceptions

Perfect Proposal

Hidden Heat

STANDALONE STORIES

All I Need for Christmas

Unashamed